GIANT TALES
APOCALYPSE
10-MINUTE STORIES

LAVA

STORM

IN THE

NEIGHBORHOOD

Professor K.R. Limn Books

CRYSTAL SWORD CHRONICLES
GRYFFON MASTER

GIANT TALES
APOCALYPSE
10-MINUTE STORIES

LAVA
STORM
IN THE
NEIGHBORHOOD

Introduction by
PROFESSOR K.R. LIMN

Professor Limn Books
Charlotte, North Carolina

Dedication

*For those shaken by earthly tremors
and for those who have seen
steam and water launched skyward
by volcanic eruptions
or witnessed hail and fiery lava
plummet to Earth,
we dedicate our stories
in acknowledgment and honor of
disaster relief workers and
first responders.*

Preface

This anthology is a work of fiction
written by twenty-three authors.
Each 10-minute story takes place
after a great earthquake has shaken
the entire Earth,
causing numerous volcanic eruptions
and multiple lava storms.
A suggested story prompt was given
in an online fiction group, writers750.com,
with the purpose of creating
a new and original short story.
LAVA STORM IN THE NEIGHBORHOOD
has twenty-three short stories
where the simple theme is *My Brother's Keeper.*
Each short story includes lava or lava rocks,
the first sign of wildlife, and a bully who is on the loose.
I asked authors to explore this setting
because even though we might feel powerless
to avoid natural disasters,
we can still help prepare
emergency responders and
accept responsibility for
the welfare of mankind.

PROFESSOR K.R. LIMN

Contents

LAVA STORM
IN THE
NEIGHBORHOOD

AFTERWORD

Randy Dutton
Shae Hamrick
Mike Boggia
Sharon Willett
Susan Davis
Laura Stafford
Lynette White
Harry Alexiou
Randall Lemon
Christian W. Freed
H.M. Schuldt
Joyce Shaughnessy
Sylvia Stein
Janet Bond
Douglas G. Clarke
Gail Harkins
Amos Parker
Paul D. Scavitto
Stephanie Baskerville
Glenda Reynolds
Rebecca Lacy
Angela Drew
Robert Tozer

Photo courtesy of NASA

Volcano Kelut (Kelud) exploded on February 13, 2014, causing an ash cloud 19 miles in height, endangering jet engines. This type of natural disaster can clog and stall aircrafts. So flights from seven airports were rerouted.

Falling ash was the biggest threat to people who live near this mountain. Evacuations enforced over 75,000 people in Indonesia to stay out of a 6-mile wide area. Among those who died, the leading causes were due to ash inhalation, shortness of breath, and collapsing buildings.

Reports noted that the falling ash had also affected farms, animals, and water supply. Damages include 3,782 houses, 20 government buildings, 251 schools, 9 hospitals, and 37 churches.

Volcanologists could anticipate this particular natural disaster 3-4 days before the eruption took place.

INTRODUCTION

You'll instantly feel the powerful theme, *My Brother's Keeper* in this apocalyptic setting. *LAVA STORM IN THE NEIGHBORHOOD (Book 1)* uncovers nature's raw power throughout the world, written by twenty-three creative fiction authors who know how to develop a great story. With all new believable tales and reasonable consequences triggered by the greatest earthquake on Earth, you will absolutely cherish the question, *Am I My Brother's Keeper?* and want to keep turning the pages for more great giant tales. See if you can find the big bad bully in each story and learn how to survive the most deadly lava storm this Earth has ever seen.

Giant Tales brings you another fantastic collection of short stories. This new series rolled out in 2014, *Giant Tales Apocalypse 10-Minutes Stories* where entertainment, action, and adventure is found. Come meet unique heroes, exciting enough you'll want to get to know them. Unleashed in a new world, characters face a challenging situation. I am proud to present to you, *LAVA STORM IN THE NEIGHBORHOOD.*

PROFESSOR K.R. LIMN

1

THE MUDPOT

by
Randy Dutton

BLURP! Hot mud splattered the long-abandoned, half-sunk Prius, its right front wheel barely touching the crumbling asphalt driveway.

"Lower the pipe!" Harry Corrade yelled across the steam-billowing pond. He slowly released his end of the scavenged pipe into the reddish gray ooze.

"Okay, my end's down!" Mary called back through the sulfurous vapor. "Can't wait to get that hot bath!"

Harry stepped over the car's restraining cable and walked around the burbling mudpot. "Well, at least something good's come from this bottomless mess." He held his breath and quickly crossed a makeshift walkway to the navigation buoy floating in the center. He turned a handle. A turbine he had installed inside started spinning. He ran back and exhaled. "Whew!" A light bulb glowed. "Okay, now we have electricity. Pump's on and your hot water's flowing!"

"Yippee!" She draped her arms around his neck and gave him a long smooch. "You're so clever to turn this smelly pit into an asset."

"And now we'll be able to grow food year-round in our heated greenhouse."

She nodded at the mineral-encrusted car. "Why don't you just cut the cable and let that rusted car sink? Consider it an offering to Vulcan," she jested. "You already pulled the batteries before the driveway collapsed."

"Placating volcano gods is low on my priorities. I'll find a use for it someday."

She took his hand and led him toward the house, but her attention was on the ocean waves. "Did 'ya ever think when we built a couple decades ago that we'd have oceanfront property?"

"From 10 miles inland and 200 feet up? Nope. And I never thought I'd have to rebuild the house after megaquakes flattened it. Who'd a thought an asteroid hitting the Pacific Rim fault line in *Chile* would cause our Olympic Peninsula to sink and the ocean to rise?"

She pouted. "For awhile, I thought we were doomed."

He grinned. "Glad we were on the front lawn when the first shock struck."

"Like nine days on a roller coaster...up, down, sideways, and plunge...I've always hated those things."

"I'm not sure which was worse...losing our home...or the forests burning."

Passing Harry's workshop, their attention turned to the direction of two gunshots echoing along the shoreline.

"Having a tyrant nearby!" she responded sourly. "Definitely worse."

"Don't worry about Hector, those were a few miles away."

Her brow lifted. "Think he found some game?"

"I dunno. I saw some deer tracks yesterday, first ones since the firestorm. But he'd shoot anything just to prevent someone else getting it."

She smiled up at him. "At least you knew how to survive and thrive." She wrapped her arm around his and leaned into him as they walked past stacked piles of volcanic ejecta— rocks that, a year earlier, had pelted all land within 200 miles of each of the 452 reawakened Pacific Rim volcanoes. "Think I'll hire you out to other survivor pockets. I could be rich!"

His nose lifted. "And what would you trade for?"

Her smile widened, and she swung her hip into his. "Well, ammunition makes good currency."

He chuckled. "You'd probably never see me again."

She stopped and continued holding his hand, forcing him to turn to her. Her brow furrowed. "You think someone would capture you?"

"These are tough times. Global population's under two billion, or so I've heard on the shortwave. A year after the asteroid and renewed volcanism, our government's barely functioning and still limited to the east coast—well, what's left after the flooding. There's hardly any infrastructure this side of the Central Time Zone."

"Think they'll ever reclaim the western US?"

He shook his head, then looked at the lightning flashes from Mount Rainier's perennial mushroom cloud, 100 miles south eastward. "I think they've given up. The Pacific now extends into California's central valley. The cities have crumbled. The roads and rails are all buckled. Bridges are down. Atmospheric dust pretty much prevents air travel and limits communications. Even a pony express would fail because the grasslands…don't have grass. Ash is too deep." He smiled affectionately at his wife. "Thankfully, we're upwind from the Cascade Mountain volcanoes and are better off than most."

"Yea, but a few thousand miles downwind from Asia's and Alaska's volcanoes. I wonder what animals survived. The diversity used to be so rich here."

He inhaled deeply then slowly exhaled. "Time will tell. At least the sea life's starting to recover."

"Not much to fish with. Except for Hector's locally built boats, I haven't seen an intact ship since the waves receded."

"Those thousand-foot tsunami waves bouncing around the oceans probably wiped most of them out, including the capacity to fix or build new ones." He looked up in thought. "Except maybe around the Black Sea. Outside of organized communities, anarchy rules."

"Don't forget our local sheriff. When that scoundrel finds out what you've created—"

"Some sheriff!" he scoffed. "Hector declared himself one only because he had more guns."

"I hear his fishing community's terrified of him. Rumor has it that he's enslaved a few guys traveling through."

"No doubt he trumped up some charges and 'arrested' them and is working them as prison laborers. Wanna bet they have technical skills he needs?"

She nodded.

Harry continued. "He believes you're either the victim—or the victimizer." He put his hands on her shoulders and pulled her close. "Don't worry, Mary. He's five miles away. We're small. I think he's got enough on his mind running roughshod over his fiefdom. And he knows we're always armed."

They stepped onto their front porch, illuminated by the late afternoon light reflecting off the ocean. She looked at their 'Welcome' doormat. "With power, we're gonna attract outliers to our little enclave. How're we going to say no to some and yes to others?"

He patted his holstered pistol. "With strict rules, and force, if necessary. We'll help those willing to work, but we certainly don't need freeloaders. I wouldn't mind getting some craftsmen with families to build here. We have a great spot for a small town and we could use the company."

* * *

The following day, the late morning sun had just peaked over the perpetual Cascade Mountain wall of smoke and illuminated the tracks in the mud. Mary stared at the human footprints heading to the forest. She put her foot next to it for comparison. Her lips pursed. *Small feet, but long pace and deep heal prints. Must be moving fast. Slack tide, prints can't be more than an hour old*, she thought. Her right hand instinctively slid into her coat pocket to touch the revolver's ivory grip. Her eyes shifted toward the jumble of downed trees, then clasped her half-full beachcombing basket tighter and briskly walked the half-mile home.

"Harry, we're going to have company," she said nervously, walking through the front door.

Her husband was at the dining room table rebuilding a Ford's generator into a water micro-turbine. He reached over his project and picked up his pistol. He released the clip, checked the chamber, reinserted the clip, and released the slide. It went into his holster. "How many?"

"Looks like someone on the run. Probably shorter than you. Came from the fish camp and ran into the dead timber."

He stood up and reached for a .30 caliber rifle pegged above the door. "Wish we had a dog. I worry about you walking the beach alone."

"Hello!" a man interrupted from beyond a yard fence.

"State your business!" Harry yelled from inside.

"Name's Freck. I need help!" A short man stepped up to the fence, his arms stretched out in supplication.

"He looks like he's in distress. Very skinny." Mary whispered from the window.

"Probably hungry and scared out of his wits. I'll venture a prisoner runaway from Hectorville." Harry whispered back sarcastically. Loudly, he asked, "What kind of help?"

"There's a lunatic after me!"

Harry grinned, and whispered to his wife, "Yep. Hector. Babe, get some food for the man, but keep your pistol concealed and ready." He stepped outside, the rifle cradled in his arms, then peered around the corner. Seeing the man was unarmed and alone, he motioned with the rifle. "Come on up to the porch."

* * *

Over the next hour, and between bites of food, Freck told the couple of his ordeal. "As a Boeing engineer I had worked on satellite GPS tracking of aircraft, so the sheriff demanded I fix all the GPS navigation gear for his fishing boats."

"What did he do when you told him you were trying to find your family?" Mary asked.

"He didn't care. Said his fishing fleet was more important than any one person."

"So he arrested you?" Her eyes widened.

"For disrespecting a public official."

Harry shook his head in disbelief. "Hector's a menace!" He looked into Freck's eyes. "How soon until the sheriff knows you're gone?"

"Probably already does. My ankle was usually shackled, but because I had to work in a confined electrical space, the watcher unclasped one end." He pulled up his pant leg to show the metal loop around an abraded ankle, the free loop tucked into a frayed sock. "I worked all night and, just before dawn, I told the guy I'd take a nap there in the cabinet. I shimmied out the other end."

Harry sighed, and Mary grimaced.

"Was it just you?" Harry asked.

"Heavens, no! There are a couple dozen prisoners. Most in the same situation. Some died in the short time I was there."

Harry's eyes narrowed. "How'd they die?"

"Some from fire, one got electrocuted, and he shot three."

"Shot?" Mary's brows lifted.

"Executed. Two for disobedience. One trying to escape."

"Under what authority does he believe he has to execute people?" Harry asked, his voice getting gravely.

"Claims he's implemented martial law."

"How many men does he have?" Harry asked sternly.

"Maybe a dozen. 'Deputies,' he calls them. I'd say they're more like psychotic opportunists."

Harry looked at Mary. "We've got a problem!"

"You think he'll come here next?"

"I'd count on it!" Harry looked at Freck's shaking hands. "Friend, we've got to hide you."

Freck's eyes were wide with fear. "He's got a couple dogs, too!"

Harry rubbed his face for a while, his eyes darting around the room for ideas. Then his eyes narrowed. "Okay, here's what we're going to do."

* * *

The afternoon sun glimmered off the rolling ocean and illuminated the underside of the dusty cloud to the east. The three were gathered in front of his small workshop. Harry wiped his dirty hands on his jeans and looked into Freck's twitching eyes. "You know what to do when I say, 'Here, take it'?"

"Yes, I'm to pull the cord that holds that pin."

"Remember, Freck. Tug hard. And don't let them see you." Freck's hands continued shaking. Harry handed him the pistol, butt first, and put it into his hand. "Here's my revolver. Know how to use it? Pull the hammer back. Use two hands and aim for their gut. Then pull the trigger. It'll have a kick."

He nodded. "What if they have their dogs?"

"The mudpot's sulfur will mask your scent."

Freck scampered into the hole and pulled the plywood camouflage over him.

"Mary, stay in the pump house. When the cable goes taut, and I say, 'drop it,' you step out of the shelter with your gun leveled at the right side man. If they start shooting, fire all your rounds from right to left, get back inside and bolt the door. Then reload. The cinderblocks will protect you."

"I'm not comfortable with you being so exposed," she said nervously.

"I figure I've got ten seconds to take control."

They turned toward the ocean when they heard the sputtering of a small motor. Four men with rifles were jumping into the shallows. Mary quickly walked into the small shelter.

Harry stood alone, looking up the beach. There were another three men walking his way. The middle man was larger than the others. Two Rottweilers led them, their noses sniffing the ground. His eyes shifted to a pebble on the ground five feet away. It centered in the dirt he had just leveled out. His hand gently wiggled the solid table to his left. His placid expression was forced. He was nervous as hell.

The large barrel-chested sheriff stopped 20 feet in front of Harry. "Corrade, I've heard about you!" The armed men spread themselves in a semi-circle with the sheriff in the middle. Hector scanned the small homestead. His eyes focused on the mudpot about a hundred feet away and the equipment arrayed around it. "A man of your tinkering talents would be useful to my town."

"Not interested," Harry responded flatly.

His men chuckled, and the sheriff snorted. "As if *that* mattered. I'm looking for an escaped prisoner."

"What'd he do?"

"Broke the rules."

"Who's rules?"

The sheriff showed a toothy grin and slightly leaned forward. "My rules."

"Well, he's not here."

Hector stepped five feet closer. "Did I say it was a *man*?"

"Isn't it? I doubt you'd bring six men with you for a woman."

"Think you're pretty smart, don't ya, Corrade?"

"Smart enough to know you don't have jurisdiction here."

The sheriff again turned and looked at the property. His grin turned malevolent. "My town hereby annexes your land all the way to that creek."

"Since law says affected landowners have a vote, I vote against it."

"This isn't a democracy, and you don't *have* a vote."

"You're abusing your power, Hector. Get off my land!"

"And you're under arrest!" The sheriff raised his rifle and stepped within ten feet.

"For what?!" Harry demanded.

"For disrespecting me. Now, hand over your pistol." Hector reached out.

"No!"

The sheriff took a step closer to within eight feet. He aimed his rifle at Harry's head. "Hand it over!"

Harry picked it out of his holster with thumb and forefinger and held it in front. "You want this?"

The sheriff grinned wider at the dangling .45 semiautomatic. He took another step forward. His feet straddled the pebble.

"Here. Take it!" Harry yelled and slammed the pistol onto the table. The sheriff's eyes gleamed, and his men chuckled.

For Harry, the next second took an eternity as the Prius, held for nearly a year by a restraining cable, was released by the pulled pin. As the heavy vehicle suddenly submerged into the volcanic pit, the cable went taut. The snare loop, positioned just around the sheriff's leg, pulled out of the loose soil. Hector was in mid-stride with his hand outstretched for Harry's weapon, when the loop tightened around the bully's ankle, yanking his feet out from under him. The sheriff yelped, then clawed the ground while being dragged ever faster toward the steaming pool. Four deputies yelled while chasing him. Two had dropped their weapons so they could grab him. The barking dogs joined the game of chase.

Harry grabbed his pistol off the table and the barrel of the sheriff's rifle lying on the ground. He flipped over his solid wood table and knelt behind it. He holstered his pistol and pulled out the shotgun taped to the underside.

The remaining two armed deputies stood dumbfounded, watching their boss being dragged, feet first, with the others in chase. For a moment, Harry's advancing shotgun didn't register with them.

"Drop it!" Harry demanded. "On the ground, hands behind your back!"

Mary appeared, her added rifle convincing them.

Hearing the sheriff's plaintive screams from near the pit, Harry quickly wrapped precut pieces of bailing wire around the deputies' wrists, then raced after the remaining four, each holding onto the sheriff's arms.

The big man's bound foot was just inches from the steaming mud. The remaining weapons were abandoned nearby. The scene was in balance, the pit not winning its prize, the man not escaping. "Corrade, you're a dead man!" the big man screamed. His beat red face stared up in agony.

Harry pondered his next move, but within seconds, nature made the decision for him. A big air bubble erupted at the surface and splattered boiling mud over the sheriff and three of his men. Their screams were accompanied by a kerplunk as they lost their grip and committed their boss to the boiling depths.

Freck now stood on the other side of the deputies nervously shaking the revolver. Harry aimed his shotgun and sternly warned two men reaching for their discarded rifles. "One more inch and I'll blow your hands off!"

Their hands withdrew. Freck retrieved the rifles and together they led the men back to the pump house.

* * *

Rain was threatening when two Rottweilers ran into the warm greenhouse, bumping and startling Mary while she was planting seeds. They scampered out. She quickly dusted herself off and nervously picked up the shotgun leaning against the table.

"Babe, I'm home!" Harry cried out as he and Frank approached.

She put the weapon down. "I thought you'd return tomorrow from Hectorville."

He hugged her. "It's now Freedom. And the townspeople gave us a small boat." He nodded to the beach.

She cocked her head, "So everything went as planned?"

"Better. They seized the remaining deputies and elected a new sheriff."

"And the prisoners?"

"All released. The town made sure those eager to leave were well-fed, and provisioned. But some opted to stay."

"Why are you grinning?"

Harry whistled a few notes, then said, "I invited some of them to find their families and move here. Some real craftsmen in the group!" The dogs ran back inside and started nuzzling her hands.

She rubbed their noses. "That's great!"

"The townspeople wanted you to have the Rotts." Harry turned and walked back outside.

She knelt down and petted the playful dogs, then looked up when her husband carried in a cage. "What's that?"

"Another gift. A breeding pair of wild rabbits! Life is returning."

An Afterword to this story is on page 237.

EMBERS FOR AMBER

by
Shae Hamrick

Amber climbed the large leaning oak, one branch at a time, listening to it creak with each step. The lava flow, cooling below, caused sweat to run down her nose. Smoke and ash in the air choked her. She wiped sweat away with the back of her hand and focused on not falling off the thick charred branch. If she could get halfway out, she'd jump to the remains of the housetop that now sat frozen in the flow, smoke rising from the remains of the walls.

Pausing and looking around, she counted herself blessed. Only three homes in her mountain neighborhood had survived the earthquake and volcano that grew out of them. Ash and lava bombs had spewed for days. Looking east, she could see the darkened land from the clouds of ash that the west winds had blown over the snow. Giant lava rocks pockmarked the middle.

She shivered as she glanced at her big brother, John. He motioned her on. Her father stood looking around from behind, his gray bangs falling in his eyes. She turned back and adjusted her balance, testing each step before moving on. She wished the lava flow had been snow instead.

The after-quakes started a snow slide the third day. She and her family hunkered down in the avalanche bunker. It was days before the sounds settled and they ventured out. The snow melted as the lava flows pulsed through the forest, catching everything on fire. Now the flames were gone and so was their store of food and water. It was head for the valley or starve.

Amber jumped onto the roof, and then she glanced toward what was left of the mountain forest.

Her foot went through the shingles. She was falling.

Panicked, Amber clawed at the roof tile as she slipped further. The hole grew larger and threatened to swallow her.

She screamed. Her vision faded. All she saw were the shingles and nothing to grab.

Both legs dangled through the roof and the heat from below burned through her shoes.

A hand grabbed her arm. She gripped the hand and looked up.

Her father lay across the roof, pulling her. "Hold on Am."

The roof bit into her waist. She screamed again, shutting her eyes against the pain.

Hands wrapped around her hips. She turned. Her brother lay across another section of roof and lifted her away from the sharp edges. Inch by inch they lifted her until soon she could get a knee up. She then scrambled across the slippery shingles to her father's side.

"Step, Am. Don't jump," John chided as he crawled closer. But he stopped when the roof creaked.

Amber gulped in air and wiped away tears. "Now you tell me."

After a short rest, they crawled to the other side of the roof. The forest still stood there. John clambered down the side.

"Let go," he said as Amber clung to the eve.

The ten-foot fall terrified her. It took all her willpower to open her hands. He caught her as she fell.

They wandered through the woods, skirting lava flows and large glowing rocks. No signs of life remained except for the trees. They found a stream but the water was heavy with ash and dead fish. They continued on.

The further they went, they found larger patches of forest untouched by the ravages of the lava storms. Amber eagerly ate at the snow, savoring the cold and the moisture. Her lips burned.

"Careful," John chastised. "You'll freeze your hands and we have no medical supplies. We should stay close to the lava flows or the cold could overcome us before we can find help."

"If any still exist," Father replied.

Amber's heart sunk. "There has to be. Surely this was only on our mountain. It couldn't have been everywhere, could it?"

John shook his head. "Have you heard any planes or helicopters? If this wasn't widespread, where is everybody?

Wouldn't they have come to see what happened if only to look for survivors?"

Amber stared. Her mind could come up with no answers.

"Really, Amber," John continued, a scowl ingrained in his face but his gaze looked away. "Of fifty families in our neighborhood alone, why has no one come looking?"

Shivering, Amber looked around her, seeing nothing but snow and trees. Where was everyone? "Maybe they think we are dead. Maybe they came earlier and we were down in our bunker. Maybe that's why we haven't seen our neighbors either. They were already rescued." She paused, grief threatening to make her eyes water again. She ducked her head. "'Cept the Pinkertons we found."

"Leave off, John," Father said, swatting the air toward her brother and moving to sit by her. "Amber, you're probably right, in part, but they should have come back and we have yet to see any signs of live animals…" He grimaced and her mind flashed to the burnt remains they had seen earlier. Her stomach turned again. "We have a long way to go yet and we don't know what we will find. Stay positive but be prepared."

Amber nodded but she was determined they would find others soon. Hope was all she had left.

"Let's get moving," John said and turned to walk down the hill and along the tree line.

Amber stood and trudged behind them. Evening was coming and they wouldn't be able to go much further. They needed to find a place to sleep soon.

Step by step she followed. The warmth of the lava, some distance off to the side, countered the cool of the winter mountain forest on the other. They hadn't brought coats as they had been destroyed when the lava flowed through their house.

Amber glanced at the large trees. They had been her friends and playmates all her life. Now, what was left of them would be their salvation.

Amber smiled. Then she bumped into John.

"Hey. Why did you stop?"

Glancing around him, she spotted a wolf.

Amber froze.

John slipped his hunting knife out. The wolf looked at each of them. Her father, his hand on the hilt of his knife, stood to the left of her and John. His face was grim and he shook his head. Everyone waited.

The wolf moved a few steps to his left and sniffed the air. His gaze never left them.

Amber held her breath, her heart stuck in her throat.

The wolf sidestepped to the left again. His ears twitched.

Why were there no others? Didn't they run in packs?

Amber swallowed hard, a gasp escaping as she took a quick breath. John flinched and her father jolted.

The wolf lowered and bared his teeth.

Amber's vision wavered and she felt light headed.

A loud bang made her jump. The wolf yelped and ran into the woods.

Falling to her knees, her heart began beating again as she watched him leave.

"Dang," a gruff shout came from behind a tree to their right. Amber turned toward the voice.

A man in a heavy coat and scraggly beard walked out, holding a rifle. "He would have been good eat'n."

"Eating," Amber exclaimed, regaining strength. "He almost ate us!"

The man smiled and tucked his gun under an arm. "Well, ya can't hold that against him. There hasn't been much prey around here of late. Everythin' dead or run off and all."

"How do you happen to be here?" Father asked, his hand still on his knife hilt.

Nodding, the man stopped, his other hand pointing back the way they had come. "I was up hunting when the world exploded 'round me. Had to hunker down for a bit and then thought would be best to head down and see what was what. Came across your tracks and thought I might be of some help."

John pushed past Amber to stand in front of her. "And so you just happened to be here to scare the wolf off at just the right moment?"

Confusion washed over Amber. This man had just saved them.

The man glanced at the ground, a grin spreading to his eyes. "Well, if ya puts it that way, suppose it do seem strange. But truth is, I was just about to catch up with ya when the wolf shows up. And I didn't shoot to scare him. I hit him. Just not well enough to kill him. 'Fraid my hands don't hold as still as they did before all this happened. Burnt them comin' down here."

Amber stood. "Oh! Let me see." She scooted around John and walked toward the man. "What's your name?"

The man looked at her, his eyes growing wide as she took his hands and turned them over. There were several burns but almost as many scars.

"Well. I'm Joshua, Miss."

Amber smiled. She liked that name. "Hi, Joshua. I'm Amber." She turned his hands over a couple of times. "These don't look so bad. You wouldn't happen to have left some food just back there would you?"

Joshua shook his head, his features drooping. "No, Miss. I was hoping ya might have some, but I see now we are all four in the same tight spot."

Her hopes dashed. The few berries and nuts they had found hadn't helped her hunger.

John came up beside her on the left and pulled her back a little. "And it could be a while before we find anything."

Joshua nodded and glanced to Amber's right. Amber turned to see her father behind them.

"We aren't but a day or two from the valley and another from the city. We can stay the night here and start again in the morning."

Joshua shook his head. "The wolf'll be back and might bring more. Come, I'll show you a better place I saw back here. And there are some roots the miss can have. My hunger can wait a day. I wanted to catch up as I knew I was close, so I didn't stop when I passed by earlier. There aren't many though, so we'll have to keep a lookout as we go tomorrow."

Amber smiled. The thought of anything to eat caused her stomach to grumble.

They followed the man up the hill and closer to the lava flows. A small rock cropping surrounded by trees had survived and made a cozy bed of leaves. "I'll take first watch," Father said, "in case the wolf returns. John, you can take the second half of the night."

John nodded, glancing at Joshua.

"I can sit a spell if you want," he offered.

Father smiled. "You sleep tonight. You can take a watch tomorrow night."

He grinned but didn't seem offended.

Amber shook her head. *That was rude of them, but at least I don't have to take a watch.*

* * *

Father woke them before the sun had risen. Joshua went and found small white tubers on the end of what looked like a weed. After he ate two, Amber tried them. They were crisp and didn't taste too bad. Father smiled at Joshua as they headed out. John, however, let Joshua lead and kept himself between Amber and Joshua.

They traveled at a snail's pace. They stopped often. Amber's legs wearied and her feet blistered. She wished she'd taken up jogging with John last spring.

They quit following the lava when it tapered off toward another hollow. As evening drew nigh, Joshua scouted ahead and found them a safe place they could sleep. Howls in the night caused Amber to shiver. The wolf had found a friend.

"They won't come close, miss," Joshua said, his face gleaming as he tended the fire they'd started. "And if they see the fire in the city, then they might come find us."

John grunted and rubbed his hands. "The birds are back and there is scurrying in the woods ahead of us, but I still haven't heard anything larger than a squirrel wandering the woods. Where could they have all gone? There isn't that much forest left."

Father shrugged. "Hopefully, we will find some people tomorrow and they can tell us. Get some sleep. I'll take first watch."

Joshua glanced in his direction. "I can take the watch, sir."

Father shook his head but grinned. "You can take last watch if John decides to fall asleep again."

"I didn't," John shouted, glancing Amber's way.

Amber stared. Had John fallen asleep yesterday?

John dug at the ground with a boot. "I just closed my eyes for a minute."

Father chuckled. "Snoring more like. I'll take first watch, John can have second, and Joshua last. If Amber gets enough rest, we might make it to the city in the morning."

Amber flushed and ducked her head. She was holding them up. "Maybe you and Joshua should go in and bring back someone. It would be faster and you wouldn't have to wait for me. And we could get some real food. No offense, Joshua. The roots are good but... you know."

Joshua nodded. "I know, miss. I would relish some real home cooked food myself."

"No," Father said. "We stay together. If the wolves decide not to keep their distance, four stand a better chance than two."

"Even so," Joshua agreed.

John scowled as he rolled over. He had pushed for her to move faster all day, when Father wasn't watching. Amber sighed and went to sleep, aching in her feet and legs. They listened to the howls of the wolves in the distance.

* * *

The next day dawned clear and bright. A warm breeze blew away the bitterness from the day before. Amber hoped they would make the city today. Exhaustion pulled at her, despite Father letting them sleep in. Joshua found more roots and a few berries on his last watch. John was up early as well and found water nearby.

They continued their trek, spirits high. They would be able to see the other side of the valley soon. Climbing the small ridge took every effort Amber could muster. As they reached the last few steps, she gained strength. John and Joshua stood looking down to the valley. Father and Amber walked out of the wood line and crested the small rise.

Amber dropped to her knees and cried.

Below, in the valley, stretched miles and miles of ash, lava, rocks, and ruin. The city and the forest were cinders and ash. The warm breeze came from across the valley.

Amber wiped away the tears to clear her vision. Only now did she realize the breeze smelled of smoke and ash. Only now could she hear the pop and crackle of burning pines and forest. In the vast waste before them nothing moved. Father grabbed her arm, lifting her to her feet.

"Come on, we go this way."

Amber stared, trudging along without any will. Following because there was nothing else to do but follow.

Her legs, her arms, her head felt weighted down. She ached for food and rest. How much further could they go?

Amber stumbled to the ground.

John knelt beside her. "Come on, sis. We can't give up."

Amber just looked at him. "Why? Where can we go now?"

Father pulled at her arm. "We go to the next town and the next and we keep going till we find someone or someplace we can rest and call home. But we keep going."

Amber shook her head and stayed put. Evening was already coming and the darkness had begun to swallow the horrible world around her. "I can't go on."

Joshua knelt next to John. "Come on, miss. We can go over here and rest for the night. It's not the best place but it's good enough. The morning will be better. You'll see."

Amber looked at his smiling face and wondered how he could be so happy. His smile wavered. He'd smiled just to encourage her this whole time.

Amber moved to his new spot and watched as John set a fire. Joshua brought back several roots and plants. Amber wasn't hungry. She lay down to sleep.

A loud crack woke her.

John sat to one side and Father spoke quietly with Joshua to the other side. Amber sighed. *Probably a dream.* She closed her eyes just as several more cracks sounded behind her. Amber sat straight up and stared into the dark.

"Amber," Father called softly behind her. "Come over here."

Amber didn't glance his direction, but crawled up on her haunches and scooted back.

Watching the dark.

Waiting for something to jump out.

Her heartbeat thumped in her ears, making it hard to listen.

Amber bumped into something behind her and jumped.

A hand stopped her from going far. Glancing back, Joshua held onto her. His eyes focused on the woods and his other hand on his rifle.

Another crack, much closer drew her back to the dark.

From the side of one of the trees, a man walked out holding a rifle, wearing a dark orange vest, and carrying a backpack.

"Man, am I glad to see you," he said, coming to a stop. He then squeezed a button on a radio attached to his backpack strap. "Central, I found them. Four survivors at forty west by twenty-five north of base." He looked back up and smiled. "We have been trying to find you since we saw your campfire last night from the watchtower. Hope you're hungry. We have a whole town of survivors waiting to welcome you."

An Afterword to this story is on page 238.

3

MY BROTHER'S KEEPER?

by
Mike Boggia

Fanny June Pruitt huddled in Gar's old Mackinaw, a sodden scarf wrapped round her head. Her dark eyes darted a frightened trapped mouse. Snow cascaded behind her. The forest threatened, gloomy under low storm clouds.

"Let the poor woman come in, Tark." Beth pushed past me and opened the door wider. "Lord, Fanny June, what are you doing out here in this storm?"

My sweet wife ushered Gar Pruitt's woman into our home. I felt my cheeks burn and fists clench as I watched Beth guide her to the fireplace and take her wet outer garments. With the skill and speed of one practiced in these situations, she brought a mug of hot coffee into the living room and handed it to Fanny June. She sank into the armchair, teeth chattering, hands trembling as she lifted the cup to her lips.

Several thoughts raced through my mind as I stared at the woman, searching for bruises on her bony arms and wizen face. What had her son of perdition husband done?

"Take her boots off, Tark. I'll bet her feet are frozen." Beth stood at the kitchen sink filling a pan with warm water.

I knelt in front of Fanny June, pulled off the worn, soggy Wellingtons and patched knee socks. Her feet were pale as the snow piling up outside the window. I messaged the icy flesh with a light touch, "What happened?"

She lowered the cup from her lips. "Gar went hunting this morning, before the storm." She took another sip of coffee and stared past me into the leaping flames. "He ain't come home, Ranger Farmer." Her eyes welled.

"Oh, you poor woman." Beth put the pan in front of Fanny June. "Dip your feet in, dear. It will feel scalding hot, but isn't. Let's get you warmed up and drive the chill away." Beth glanced at me. "We need to do something."

I got to my feet and looked into the mudroom where my parka, snowsuit and Sig M400 hung. Memories rushed back from two years ago and I automatically rubbed my left shoulder. The bullet wound still ached in inclement weather. How ironic, Gar Pruitt, poacher, wife beater, drunken piece of scat, lost in a blizzard. Had nature dealt her own hand of harsh justice?

Gar and I were sons of lumbermen whose careers ended when the local mill folded and our little town threatened to flicker out of existence. Dad didn't know the word quit and used his skills with wood to begin a rustic furniture factory in an abandoned barn. He employed six of his friends the first year. By the end of the fourth year, thanks to help from the local banker, he negotiated a contract with a department store. This enabled him to hire the remaining men of the locality seeking employment.

Gar followed the same path as his father, the town drunk, who lost every job he held. Dad gave them jobs. Two weeks later, Dad came home shaking his head. Unable to tolerate their poor work ethics and habit of nipping from the bottle during lunch break, he had fired them. "I don't need their kind of liability," he growled.

Older brother, Jessie, inherited Dad's wood crafting talent. He took over the business when Dad retired. I loved the land, saw man's destruction of the natural resources, and with Jessie's help, went to college to become a forest ranger. After five years, I returned home, in charge of Rocky Ridge Mountain Reserve. Gar and I found ourselves on opposite sides of the law. The narrow gulf between us grew to Grand Canyon proportions.

Two years ago in mid-June, I caught Gar with a poached doe and fawn in the back of his pickup. He snatched his 30.06 and fired from the hip. I returned fire as his bullet ripped through my shoulder. He escaped, unharmed. Deputies tracked him to his root cellar and arrested him.

Gar's trial lasted two days. He faced charges from the sheriff for attempted murder, probation violations, and poaching. At the prosecutor's request, the judge reduced that charge. His last words to me, as deputies dragged him out of court to serve his sentence, were, "Next time, I'll aim better."

Threats go with the job. Gar's promise, spoken in a hushed voice, was an icy calculated promise that ran through my mind almost every day and haunted my dreams.

Two months ago, the court system released Gar on parole.

It didn't take long for him to return to his old ways. I would have to confront him and that left a sick feeling in the pit of my gut. Fanny June's thin voice broke through my thoughts.

"Officer Farmer, he ain't poachin'. He got him a license on opening day."

I nodded at her. Provisions of his parole forbid ownership or possession of a firearm. Gar had told several people in town that he planned to get even with that terrible ranger and someone should tell me to make out my will. A day of reckoning or ambush was eminent.

"He might be home by now, Fanny June. It must have taken you a good hour to walk here."

She looked at the clock above the mantel. "Hour and a half."

"Your husband will be furious if supper's not on the table."

She cringed and I regretted adding to her fears. Fanny June's father forced Gar to marry her when he learned she was pregnant. She lost the baby. Gossip said he'd beaten the child out of her, though no proof existed. Her choice to continue to live with Gar, instead of her parents, was the lesser of two hells. Her father was a wife and child beater, though neither his wife nor children ever spoke out against him.

"I left a pot of stew simmering on the back of the stove and a note telling him where I went."

I peered into the falling snow from the front window. Gar might come here under a head of steam, ready to blow, then again, he might never return. "It's not getting any better out there, Fanny June. I'll ride my snowmobile to your place and see if he's home. If he isn't, I'll call search and rescue to see if they can do anything tonight, though I doubt they'll go out in this weather."

The drive to Pruitt's cabin took double the normal time, proved uncomfortable and nonproductive. Darkness swallowed the forest. A blizzard can disorient the most experienced woodsman.

Beth met me at the door of our mudroom as I entered from the garage. I shook my head. Fanny June's eyes filled with tears at the news he hadn't returned home.

"Did he mention where he was going to hunt?" I asked.

"He'd been scouting around Bottomless Swamp and Lost Lake. I guess he went there. He said there were lots of deer signs around Brayburn Meadows."

The Lost Lake locale posed numerous challenges for search and rescue. A haven for deer and other wild creatures, it defied human intrusion. Tangled vines and thick brush grasped legs. Open areas hummocked with tufts of reeds and grasses floating on a mucky morass tried to suck trespasser into their depths. It remained treacherous even when the rest of the valley froze solid. Dotted with warm springs, the mud and ice never became thick enough to support a man's weight.

Lightning torched a ten-acre parcel of the swamp twenty-three years ago, creating Brayburn Meadows. Gar and I went there as teens, using the scorched land for a science project. Gar wrote a term paper describing poisonous snakes. I did mine on the ecological impact of the fire. The only safe way to reach the meadow was a treacherous path we'd named Dead Buck Trail.

I went into my office, closed the door and called Mitch Rogers, head of search and rescue. The teams would start in the morning, weather permitting. Did selfishness prompt me to keep the prime search area to myself, or something sinister? I removed my Sig P226 from the lock box and cleaned it. I repeated the procedure with the M400 rifle. I sighted it and visualized Gar's evil face as I squeezed the trigger.

* * *

Morning brought a lull in the storm. The forecast called for another blizzard and colder temperatures in early afternoon. I told Beth and Fanny June I'd head for the staging location to meet with search and rescue. I drove the Polaris out of the garage and, instead, steered for Bottomless Swamp and Dead Buck Trail.

Mitch contacted me as I topped a ridge overlooking the swamp and lake in the valley. I had a head start, no need to lie when I told him where I planned to search. He wished me luck and said they'd be moving in my direction.

I found Pruitt's Ski Doo parked facing the way he'd come. He'd headed into the swamp on foot. The unstable ground prevented taking snow machines beyond that point. I donned my snowshoes, backpack, and slung the rifle over my shoulder. With one last sweeping look at the tangled landscape ahead, I followed the trail toward the fire-scarred hunting ground. The blizzard obliterated Pruitt's tracks. Silence, not a bird chirped. The soft snow muffled sound. I could hear my heart pound from the effort of pushing through the drifts.

Every few yards I stopped, listened, and looked; no sign of Pruitt.

The acrid smell of smoke tainted the ozone charged air. Someone had built a fire. I moved with caution. Silence. A slight breeze brought the odor, stronger now. To my left I spied an uprooted pine, an ideal shelter. I reached for the Sig and reconnoitered around it. A small patch of neon pink showed through a pile of snow. The remains of a fire, chunks of charred wood and ash lie a few feet away. It gave its last heat hours ago. I dug the hump from its insulating blanket.

Gar Pruitt's life ebbed from a stiff, comatose body. My shoulder throbbed as I cocked the Sig. No, common sense warned me. They'd know he didn't pose a threat. I removed the layer of insulating snow and knew he'd die in minutes. I holstered the Sig, contacted Mitch, and told him I was in the swamp. Mitch grumbled that Ted's machine had mechanical problems, then George tipped over his Arctic Cat and injured his leg. After two false starts, they were driving full throttle in my direction

I glanced at my watch. The elements could claim Pruitt's life in less than ten minutes. I took a sip of hot cocoa from my thermos and let nature do her work. Mitch's arrival would be in time to help me drag Pruitt's corpse to the snow machines.

* * *

Mitch, George, and Ted sat in front of the fire, feet warming and stomachs satiated with hot coffee laced with whisky. Beth bustled in the kitchen, cooking dinner.

Mitch waved to her. "Come sit with us for a few minutes, darlin'. You've been busy since we got back. Supper can wait."

Beth perched on the armrest of the sofa, beside me, her hand on my shoulder. She smiled at me. My heart made a strange jump and I stared into the fire, reliving the forty-five minutes it took the search and rescue team to reach me. After they arrived, events blurred. I never felt so numb and still felt frozen to the core.

"You should have seen your guy." George pointed at me. "Had a fire blazing, lots of heat, him in his skivvies, with Pruitt wrapped up in his clothes. Tark saved that worthless rat's butt, at the risk of his own life. Your husband's a bigger man than we are. We'd have let the guy freeze."

Beth's arm tightened around my shoulders and her lips brushed my cheek. It's my privilege to care for him, even though he hates me. One day we must answer to a greater power and I'll be able to answer honestly, when asked, "Tark, were you your brother's keeper?"

An Afterword to this story is on page 239.

4

WE CAN'T FEED THEM

by
Sharon Willett

She stared out the soot-stained window barely able to see the house across the street. The river of lava that separated them no longer sent pillars of smoke puffing into the gray sky. She flashed her gaze to the right thinking she'd seen movement. Impossible.

"Dean, I still don't see him, not even the dog," she spoke to an empty room.

From a room behind the curtain, Dean hollered, "Hey, I'm getting some static on this radio. Eleanor, come in here and hold this antenna."

"In a minute. I thought I saw something."

There'd been several nice homes with large country lots on either side of them. Now the land was broken with nothing but deep chasms holding no bottom. It was as if these homes were the only two left on Earth. She gazed right again sensing movement. A huge man stumbled along out of nowhere. No, as he drew closer she could see it was a young man carrying a small boy.

"Dean, he's got blood running down his face," she blurted out.

"What are you talking about?" The bulk of a man ripped back the curtain and limped to the window pushing her out of the way. He looked back at her as she reached for the door handle. "Get away from the door."

"He's hurt and there's a child."

"Remember what we talked about? We can't feed everyone. There's only so much food in storage."

"You don't know. You haven't been in the basement for years and I can't turn them away." She opened the door and offered what she could of a welcome smile. "Come in, you're hurt."

She reached to take the boy, but the young man pulled him tighter against his chest. "I saw the smoke from your fire. Do you have anything you could feed him?"

"Yes, of course, but first let's get you cleaned up." She glanced up at her husband then back to the young man. "What's your name?"

"Ben, and this is my son, Derek. Thank you for letting us in." Ben glanced around the open kitchen and living room. His eyes rested on the large kettle in the fireplace.

"Dean, will you take them back to get cleaned up while I get some stew for them?"

"Not much water left," Dean grumbled, but drew aside the curtain, which blocked off the rest of the house.

The charred kettle rested on blazing coals that had been pulled toward the front of the fireplace while at the back, tongues of fire danced around the log Dean had recently added. Eleanor dipped the ladle in and filled a bowl. Then she heard a soft rapping.

Eleanor opened the door to a teenaged girl lying in a pile on the doorstep. She appeared barely strong enough to lift her hand to knock. Dean flew out from behind the curtain and threw a bucket of water into the fireplace dousing the fire.

"Ben told me there are more coming this way," Dean stammered but stopped at the sight of his wife dragging the girl in. "No, not another one to feed."

Eleanor helped the girl onto the chocolate brocade couch and pulled a blanket around her. "Did you ruin the stew with that water? What did Ben say?"

"Ben? He told me that they've made a bridge over the chasm and more people are headed this way. I had to put the fire out so they won't know we're here. No more people. We can't feed them."

"We have plenty," Eleanor pleaded.

Ben and Derek sat on one of the recliners directly in front of the bookcase that covered one whole wall. Eleanor could clearly see it was just a scratch on Ben's cheek. She handed them a bowl of stew and took the other bowl to the girl. "What's your name, honey?"

"Becky," she mumbled. "What's happening?"

Eleanor wiped the dazed girl's hands and face then handed her the bowl.

"Six days ago, the day after the earthquakes, I talked with a guy in California over the short-wave radio," Dean began. "He said everyone's dead. It started with quakes that leveled whole towns, even LA. From great splits in the earth they saw mountains of lava bubble up and burn everything that hadn't already fallen into the chasms created by the quakes.

"Sounds like what happened here," Ben said. "You might expect that in California, but not here in Michigan."

"He said he'd talked to someone in Mississippi and another way over in Europe, all with the same story," Dean said.

Becky began to cry, sobbing hysterically.

"Can we stop this kind of talk for now?" Eleanor ran her fingers through the girl's hair massaging her scalp to no avail. "What's wrong, honey?"

"The bridge…it fell and took them all. My mom, she's gone," Becky screamed pulling her legs up and curling her body into a fetal position.

Dean slammed his fist against the wall. "For crying out loud, it's been a week and not a peek of the old guy. Now he wants to join the party." Eleanor joined Dean at the window to see their neighbor, Mark, waving a white flag from the front door.

"What can we do? How can we get across that stream of hot lava to help him?" Eleanor asked. Her attention switched to Ben as he carried Derek to the couch.

Ben stood over Becky. "He's cold. Can he lie next to you?"

She nodded her head, so he tucked the boy in next to the still shaking girl and joined Dean and Eleanor at the window.

"Lava is hot below, but the surface has formed a thick crust. I'll have to watch where I step, but I can help," Ben said.

Eleanor pointed to the now quiet girl. "Smart move, Ben. Her motherly instincts will make her think of the boy instead of the horrors she's faced."

Ben smiled and grabbed the cane that leaned against the recliner on his way out the door. Dean and Eleanor watched the brave young man shuffle through the ash, test the lava crust, and gingerly make his way across. Mark flung his arms around Ben then gestured wildly. Eleanor couldn't help but wonder where Mark's dog was. She hated that dog. It had barked and snarled at her every day for the last two years. When she tended her garden, walked to the car, and especially when she went to the mailbox.

Evening descended quickly against a backdrop of smoke and ash. Ben and Mark made their way back without incident. Eleanor filled another bowl of stew for her now silent but hungry neighbor. She busied herself by washing the dishes and putting them all away. Dean built a roaring fire to rid them of the chill that October night.

"Aren't you afraid someone will see?" Eleanor asked.

"They can't see the fire and it's too dark to see the smoke," he said. "We'll all have to sleep in here to keep warm. That's why the blanket's over the hallway entrance, to keep the warmth in here. We have lots of sleeping bags and blankets."

He sat in his recliner and pulled up the footrest. "Good night."

Derek tottered over to the bookcase and pulled a book too big for him to carry so he pushed it to the big man in the recliner. "Read to me," the boy demanded.

Dean picked up the large tome and said, "Well, you've got good taste kid." He pulled the boy into his lap along with the book, *Birds of America* by John James Audubon.

"You know it's been strange without any animals or birds. I don't think Earth can survive without them," Eleanor said, as she pulled up a blanket and slid deeper into the other recliner.

Becky sat up. "In school they say we need the insects to pollinate the flowers and trees."

"You won't see any birds or flying insects until the ash clears from the sky," Mark said, shaking out a sleeping bag.

"There's hope. On my way here I saw a fox. Just for a split second, but if one species can make it so can the others," Ben said.

Derek reached over, took Dean's hand, and placed it on the book. They began leafing through the pages with Derek asking the name of each bird.

Dean rose early to tend the fireplace. Eleanor made coffee and instant milk to serve with the remainder of the warmed up stew. Becky stirred her food over and over. Everyone else devoured his breakfast.

"Don't play with that food," Dean roared.

"I can't eat stew again." Becky dissolved into tears.

"Oh, how typical, the beggar is picky." Dean looked adamant, maybe even judging, but Eleanor knew it as his mask, armor for something deeper. "We haven't much, so eat what you're given."

Becky pointed at Eleanor and said, "If it weren't for her goodness, we'd all be lost."

A nervous giggle escaped Eleanor's lips. "We have plenty, but none to waste, my dear. Please eat," she urged, then turned her attention to Mark. "Where's your dog?"

Mark grunted.

"What happened to the dog?" she asked again.

Mark lowered his head and whispered, "I ate him."

Eleanor gasped.

"I hadn't done any shopping. I had nothing. We were both going to die, so I ate him on the fifth day." A tear streamed down his rugged cheek. "I didn't think I could make it over here, besides you both hated my dog."

"Well—" Eleanor stuttered.

"Don't lie," Mark interrupted. "I know you hated the dog, but he was a good dog only trying to protect his home."

"What are you talking about, old man?" Dean stomped over. "Protect his home? From us? We wouldn't do anything to you or your dog."

"The dog didn't know that. He only knew it was our house and you weren't part of it."

Dean cleared his throat, his look softened. "You did what you had to do. Not everyone packs food away. We probably wouldn't have either but for the insistence of the church folk and the fact that our boys are such good hunters."

Eleanor felt her throat thicken at the mention of their sons. They only lived on the other side of town, but didn't have a short-wave radio like their dad had asked them to get. They were smart boys. They would be fine.

"There are some of the others," Ben said. He stood by the window pointing.

Dean hobbled to the window cursing all the way. He saw one of them point up at the roof. He'd made the fire without even thinking about the smoke drawing people. "Turn them away. When they get close enough, you just tell them they have to go. We can't feed anymore. Never mind, I'll get the gun." He turned to leave the room.

"Stop. That's crazy talk. We can, we must, and we will help others," Eleanor spoke in a voice as soft as silk but firm. She went to her husband to soothe his fear. "We will need them."

"I must be in a nightmare," Dean said. "We have the whole winter before us with very little food. How will we survive if we try to feed everyone? Take a head count, Eleanor, we have six now and there's five more headed this way. I won't allow it."

"Honey, I want you to see something. Do you think you can make it downstairs?" Eleanor led him down one step at a time with Dean careful to not depend on his bad knee. The rest followed. Eleanor flicked on the light. Everyone gasped. Eleanor smiled.

Rows and rows of see-through storage bins chock full of food packed floor to ceiling, filling the entire length and breadth of the basement. There were also stacks of bottled water, boxes of canning jars, cases of cleaning supplies, medicines, and toiletries.

"I told you her goodness would save us all." Becky smiled at Eleanor.

Derek ran laughing down the rows and back again. "Yay, now gives me a wagon so I can shop."

Everyone laughed.

Eleanor pulled Dean near and said, "But that's not the best. She popped the lid on a bin and opened it to reveal hundreds of packages of seed. "It will take all of us."

An Afterword to this story is on page 240.

5

IN THE LIGHT OF A QUAKE

by
Susan Davis

Dogs barked and howled in the distance, a lot of them, startling me awake. It took a moment to get my bearing and then I remembered, Addison Benderson, a new name, a new life and the fifth day of my honeymoon.

Stretching, I sat up on the rock-hard mattress and noticed my groom, Zane, had gone missing. He probably left early to catch us some Blue Gill. The *Trail's Happy Ending Resort & Cabins* webpage bragged about the fishing and excellent wooded hiking trails at Lake Morehead, so Zane and I jumped right into reserving it for two weeks. Dad gave us his boat to use.

Crawling out from beneath the covers I moved to the open window. Dawn barely filtered through the trees on the backside of the small cottage, hard to see if anything moved, but the howling continued at a greater distance, like all the dogs or coyotes in the area collected and ran off together.

Suddenly, wind blasted through the screen, whipping and snapping the curtains out like a flag. *Wow, what a weird force of wind.* It made me think a storm brewed close, but I didn't recall hearing about any acclimate weather for Northern Michigan.

I stepped across the cool wooden floor, pulled on my long sweater that hung on a peg by the door, turned on the porch light and sauntered out. The cottage protected me from the cold gusts, but white caps slashed across the lake in crazed chaos. Dad's boat bobbed in the middle of it all.

On instinct I ran inside to grab our binoculars and returned, searching for Zane. He wasn't in the boat or near it in the water. Panic knotted my throat and punched through my stomach. *Oh, God, no, I need to get out there.*

My first thought was run to the resort store and office. Only I had no idea of time, and the door was locked. A sign on the door listed the hours as 8:00 a.m. to 9:00 p.m. Then, I saw another card stuck in the window, 'Check back in few days.'

Really? What does that mean?

My mind spun as I rushed down to the water, looking for any moored boat. There, about four docks away, I saw one thrashing up and down. By the time I reached the dock with my sweater pulling and flapping like wings, the boat had taken on too much water, whether from damage or the sloshing waves, it barely floated.

"Zane!" I screamed his name, running back and forth along the water as if caught in an unending nightmare.

A furious rumble came from the other side of the lake, vibration beneath my feet made me fall. I looked across the water and watched the entire shoreline of trees and homes lift from one side to the other, like a wave in a stadium. The ground continued to shake under me and I couldn't stand. Questions piled inside my head. Nothing like this had ever occurred in Michigan.

Then, I saw a hand reach up from the dock. Tripping and stumbling, I moved over the beach and up the dock, grabbing the hand before it sank into the water. I held tight with both hands, determined not to allow him to slip away. Getting some leverage with my feet against a post and using all of my strength, I hauled Zane over the edge. His forehead was bruised and bleeding. He wore a life-vest, something he seldom used, but most likely the reason he'd made it back. His body shook as he gagged for air.

Another tremor shook the dock. Zane still hadn't opened his eyes.

"Zane, we need to move. Wake up."

His eyes opened, but didn't focus on me. He turned his head to throw up, water gushed from his mouth and nose, making him gag some more.

The end of the dock broke loose and crashed into the tumultuous water. Rain poured from the sky, black drops, like mud. I curled an arm around Zane's waist and dragged him over the shifting wood, inch by inch toward land. My knees kept slipping, collecting slivers, cuts, and the black substance now coated everything, including me and Zane.

Wasn't positive if we'd reached solid ground as everything moved. My muscles strained hauling Zane but I didn't slow down. Deep inside I knew we needed to get away from the water. Then a horrid cracking, shattering of wood had me looking around and behind us. The dock ripped away and sucked into the water and by the sound of it, all the docks met the same fate.

"Zane, talk to me," I screamed, slapping him across the face to bring him around. Nothing. His vacant stare drove through my heart.

Where is everyone? Why isn't anyone helping us? Heavy dark rain came down even thicker than before. I'd never seen anything like it, so slick we were sliding back toward the ominous lake.

Something hit my arm, a rope. I looked in the direction it came from but could see nothing except a blanket of black rain. I wrapped the thick rope around Zane, under his arms and tied it. Then I gave the rope a yank, like a fish caught on a hook. We slid over the mud, gaining distance from the turbulent water.

A man in his mid-thirties pulled me up onto the porch of our rental and we both helped get Zane. I felt for Zane's pulse. It banged strong against my fingers.

"Name's Mr. Trail."

He must be the owner of the place and knew who we were.

"What are you two doing out in this mess? Most everyone left during the night." He stared at me like I was an idiot.

"Zane and I had music going last night." I thought about our night together, why we didn't hear people pack up and leave. *But our window was open.* Then I realized Zane must have opened the window this morning. We'd closed it last night, not wanting to share our amorous behavior. My face heated.

The guy growled. "Never mind, it doesn't matter. We need to get out of here before—"

Suddenly, everything stopped, all sound, the rain, the wind, and as if in slow motion Mr. Trail and I watched all of the water in the lake form a giant tidal wave across the other side. A wall of water stood high, like a huge mountain range. Then before it slammed forward, another thunderous cracking roar and the ground shook so hard, Mr. Trail and I joined Zane on the floor of the porch.

The wretched sound deafened. I covered Zane's right ear with my left and used my hands for Zane and my other ears. Just when I thought the noise would never end, it stopped. The ground rested. Mr. Trail and I looked out over the lake to find a great chasm, no water and all of the houses around the lake had disappeared with the exception of my rental and Mr. Trail's store.

"Omigod, everything's gone." Mr. Trail's mouth went slack, tears filled his eyes. Then he turned to me, with the strangest expression on his face, like maybe he blamed me for what just happened.

An acrid odor filled the air, sulfur, and more rumbling from below, inside the chasm.

"Come on, I've got an ATV parked behind the store. Maybe we can get to it." Mr. Trail hauled Zane up, throwing Zane's arm over his shoulder. I did the same on Zane's other side, and we staggered and slipped over the muddy rippling ground.

Thank goodness the store remained intact. Mr. Trail took us behind it, near the open-topped vehicle that looked more like a military jeep.

"Get in the back. I need to grab a few supplies." He ran off leaving me with the job of getting Zane into the seat. It took a lot of effort pulling him in without injury. I sat back, tears dripping down my face, with Zane's head in my lap.

Realization hit me. I hadn't even grabbed my phone or any of our clothes. My mind reeled, unable to think past the moment. *Why didn't we know about this major seismic event?* I had been so focused on our wedding and honeymoon. Didn't take time to watch news or listen to anything negative from our friends. I was raised to instill only positive thoughts.

Scanning the area, I saw all the devastation. Mom, Dad, my in-laws, our family and friends, all hours away in Southern Michigan, had they suffered similar incidents?

Mr. Trail threw a few big canvas bags into the front seat and jumped behind the steering wheel. The engine started right up and we peeled down the narrow lane. I looked back in time to witness Mr. Trail's store explode into a ball of fire. I turned to see him watching it from the rearview mirror, and thought it strange a faint smile etched across his face.

"Where are we going?"

His focus moved, now glaring at me in the rearview. "Don't worry your pretty little head. I've got a safe place about two hours away from any seismic activity. Seems all the volcanic stuff is west of Michigan. Ash fallout caused the black rain. Flooding took out large cities south of us."

"Was there flooding in Michigan?" I knew we had some major rivers, plus we're surrounded by great lakes. The jeep snaked around a fallen tree and we came out of the forest onto a paved road.

"Yep, but can't tell you any exact locations since I'm without my CB-radio. Satellite systems keep going down for any news coverage." He messed with the radio and got only static.

The ATV hit a deep hole. I grabbed the door handle and Zane's arm, but the force jerked me from the seat. Zane dropped onto the floor in a heap. Right after, Mr. Trail came to a stop in the middle of the road. He jumped out and flung the back door open. "Get out."

"What? Here? In the middle of nowhere?" I saw Zane's eyelashes flutter. "Zane needs medical help."

"Yep, maybe you'll get lucky and find someone else on this road." He yanked me out, and then grabbed Zane under the arms, hauling him out.

"Why did you help us at all?" Frustration racked every cell in my body until all I wanted to do was punch this mean man.

Without answering, he tossed one of the bags out and drove away, leaving me in the middle of the road with Zane and the bag at my feet.

Zane opened his eyes and looked up at me. "Addison?"

Folding to my knees, I bent over and hugged him. "You're back. Oh, my, gosh, you had me so scared." He broke away.

"Where are we?" He sat up and looked around.

"Do you think you can walk? We should probably get off the road." I helped him up and dragged the heavy bag. As we walked, Zane stood taller, apparently gaining his strength. We stopped at a fallen tree on the side of the road and leaned against it. He looked at me as if in disbelief.

"I couldn't get the boat motor to start. Darkness came in from the west, then a wind kicked up and the water started churning, pulling the boat farther and farther away from shore. So eerie, I put on the life vest. Right after, the waves got so bad the boat tipped me right out." Zane's brows furrowed. "The last thing I remember is I needed to get back to you. I swam hard, toward what I thought was our place, and then like a beacon I saw a light. I knew it was you, Addison."

Ah, yes, I remembered turning on the porch light, could that be what Zane saw? It suddenly hit me how close we came to losing our lives. I sank to the ground and Zane settled next to me. I told him everything that had happened.

"So, what did Mr. Trail leave us in that bag?"

Opening it, I pulled out *my* jewelry box full of my great grandmother's antique jewelry, Zane's leather coat, my laptop, clothing, a clock, and shoes.

"Our stuff...from our house. We were robbed. By the owner of the resort?"

Everything from the last few hours washed through my mind, shaking my body from the enormity of it. Zane wrapped his arms around me, making me feel safe, secure.

"Sounds like Mr. Trail saw the light, also. What do you think, Addison?"

Maybe he did and decided to begin somewhere else. Perhaps that explained his smile when his place exploded.

I gazed up at Zane. "I'm thinking...what a way to begin a lifetime together."

"Yeah, and it looks like we have quite a hike ahead of us." Zane's lips brushed mine, and he stood, hauling me up with him. "We'd best get started."

Just then a DNR truck pulled up and two Rangers climbed out. "Are you Addison and Zane Benderson?"

We nodded.

"We got a call a while ago with your coordinates saying you might need some medical attention."

An Afterword to this story is on page 241.

6

FAIR MEADOWS ESTATES

by
Laura Stafford

"Safest neighborhood around," the realtor had said of the gated community with its manicured lawns and perfect gingerbread cardboard cutout houses.

He was right, Jeff thought now as he surveyed the suburbs beyond the wrought iron gates that had melted into an unrecognizable hunk of metal. Three houses stood on a low knoll, surrounded by fiery devastation. Black boulders hissed steam, covered by a fine layer of soft grey ash that fell from the black sky endlessly—an oasis in an alien landscape.

A layer had accumulated on his head and shoulders as he stood on the balcony overlooking the crushed suburb beyond his doorstep. *King of the hill,* he thought and made a muffled guffaw of a laugh.

"You shouldn't stay out so long!" Amy yelled from behind him, and slammed the door with a rattling of glass.

She was right. He slid in the door, opening it only as far as he had to and closed it quickly. Amy was on the other side of the room pulling clothes on. She was dressed like a soldier with hair pulled back in a little bobbed ponytail, pants tucked into her boots, and a turtleneck pulled all the way up to her chin.

"Where are you going?" he asked.

"The Gleasons," she said. "To get some of their stuff."

"Well, wait for me and we'll be able to bring back more."

"No," she hummed. "I need you to bring in wood and keep the fireplace going. It's getting low. And I need you to go to the Readings and get more water. I'm thinking we should get whatever perishable food is left first. Then we can go back tomorrow and get the heavy stuff."

He eyed her with admiration. Amy was the voice of solidarity and reason. She had stuck by him when they made the decision to weather out the eruption, knowing their chances of surviving were slim. She had held his hand as they watched the neighborhood slowly evacuate, one family after another, to huddle together and await the impending disaster.

It had all happened so fast. The earth rumbled low and slow for several days, and the town had laughed. Old Smokey had been dormant for years, only occasionally belching a puff of smoke or a murmur of moving gas.

Then the geologists came and ran tests. They said it was going to blow, that the townspeople should evacuate. The smartest left early and probably got out of town safely. The rest headed to the gathering spots, not knowing where to go, knowing that there was no time to go anywhere anyway.

Then suddenly the earth shook and a loud explosion rocked the town and all the world beyond. Like Mount St.

Helens, the top of Old Smokey blew off into the air and rained down in flaming boulders the size of Buicks. The school was crushed. The firehouse was buried under a layer of tuff and siliceous debris. Buildings smoked and burned in the distance.

And yet this little knoll was spared. Jeff was spared. Amy was spared.

And he couldn't have been more thankful.

He would do what Amy asked, knowing that even as the world crumbled around her, she set her mind to moving forward.

She kissed him briefly, pulled on her gas mask, and bounced out the door.

* * *

The Readings house was kitschy country decor, cutesy knick-knacks, eucalyptus hanging from the corners and the ceiling, and red-checkered couches with knitted afghans precisely placed to look casually thrown.

Jeff couldn't stand the smell or the dust-collecting clutter but as it turned out, the Readings were also apocalyptic hoarders. Because they were old, Amy had thought they would be more likely to leave a door unlocked or a window open. So after the worst of the flaming debris had finally stopped raining havoc, he and Amy headed over to their house with thick Carharts pulled over their heads. Even still, Amy got a nasty burn on her arm and Jeff had a speckling of raw open wounds up his shin.

When they had first walked in to the quaint country cottage, they had both laughed at the poor Readings until they fell over on the couch together. There they kissed like it would be their last time, and certainly there was no way to know that it wasn't.

Then they made a full search of the house. In the basement, they met a stockpile of food, water and supplies. There were batteries, a transistor radio, blankets, games, a generator, and gasoline. Over the last 24 hours, the two of them had moved most of it to their own modestly decorated home on top of the hill.

He gathered the rest of the water now. There were gallon jugs that he loaded into an old wagon outside, where they were slowly blanketed in ash and soot while he went in and out, in and out.

He was breathless walking around with the gas mask on. He could only imagine what it would be like to breath the putrid chemical soup of air for any amount of time. Even just a quick opening of the door gave him a headache.

Once the load of water was safely in the house, Jeff stoked the fire and brought in the firewood. He couldn't believe how thankful he was for a simple fireplace. Again, Amy's choice in all of her God-given wisdom. Jeff thought back now to the tour.

* * *

The realtor had beamed with pride at the marble encased fireplace with its wide mantle. "It's the only house on the block with such a nice fireplace," he said. "Imagine sitting here with a good book or a nice glass of wine." Jeff looked off out through the window wistfully.

"I don't want a fireplace," Jeff whispered to Amy in the hallway. "It's so messy, and we'll have to buy firewood. It's not like we can go out to that little patch of trees by the stream and cut firewood."

"But maybe later we'll want to," she looked at him deeply. "Like at Christmas time when the children are opening presents."

Jeff saw the look in her eyes, her sight on the coming years that would bring love and children and happiness to this house. In her eyes, Jeff saw their future.

They bought the house that day.

* * *

Amy had yet to return. He poked at the fire and thought she was taking too long.

He went to the back door and saw her footprints in the ash leading to the Gleason's side door to his right. He followed them.

To his left he heard something like a squeal, down the hill near the trees that lined the stream. The sound of the stream had stopped yesterday. He saw a flash of something in his peripheral but when he turned to look, it was gone. The squirrels, the bunnies that populated the backyard in the mornings, and even the occasional deer had fled long before the actual eruption. Wiser than the humans, they knew to leave at the first sign of danger and did not pine over nonsense. Survival was their only thought.

The side door was ajar and led into a mudroom, which directly opened into the kitchen. The Gleasons were a young couple. Their house reflected their modern style—stark, sparse, organized, and spotless. The kitchen drawers had been ransacked and the refrigerator was hanging open still.

Jeff called out. "Amy? Amy!"

To the left was a large formal dining room, untouched, and beyond that an immaculate living room with white carpets and black leather sofas. No drawers or cabinets or any place to stash anything. This room too, was untouched. The front door locked.

"Amy! *Amy!*"

Back in the kitchen, Jeff observed the scene. Although the drawers had been pulled and there were things strewn about the counters, there were bags packed neatly on the table, ready to be carried back like a normal grocery shopping trip. There was another door next to the stove that led out into the garage.

"Amy!"

She wasn't in the garage. But the door to the yard stood open. There were tracks leading out, a definite set of footprints and two long ditches on either side - like she pulled the wagon out the door. *Do the Gleasons have a wagon?* Jeff wondered absurdly.

He walked over for a closer look. He glanced at the security system controls, dark and useless without electricity, or phone or anything. *Safest neighborhood in the suburbs*, he thought.

He looked out into the snowing ash. If it weren't for the devastation it covered, it would have almost been beautiful.

The footprints weren't Amy's, of that he was sure. They were as big as his own. A man's feet.

Directly on the heels of that realization, Jeff's mind connected another dot. The ditches weren't tire tracks, they were footprints—the footprints of his wife being dragged from the house.

He bolted out the door.

Jeff followed the tracks, which led to the trees. His heart was bounding along with his leaping run. It did no good to try and call out with the gas mask on. The wind was deafening in his ears and he could barely see through the whipping grey tornadoes.

He was almost on top of her before he recognized the white mound as a person. Head hanging, white with ash, covered with little piles on her shoulders, Amy sat in front of a tree with her hands behind her back, as if she were dozing there.

He stopped abruptly. She was tied up. *Tied up.*

Something hit him in the temple, but keeping Amy in his eyesight, he threw up a defensive arm. Another blow landed on his wrist and he cried out a muffled response, but managed to stay on his feet, turning towards the perpetrator.

It was Roger Gleason. No mask. No covering. His face was red with bursting blood vessels like an alcoholic. His eyes reflected the ash and they chilled Jeff. They looked cold and crazed.

Jeff lifted his mask. "Roger, it's me. Jeff. From next door. Roger."

Roger ran at him like a linebacker and grabbed him into a bear hug, pulling him nose-to-nose. His breath stank and his eyes had crust in the corners. "Good!" he cried. "You're here! You can help!"

He leapt towards Amy and shook the ash from her head.

"Roger! What are you doing?"

Roger just laughed. Jeff could see Amy trying to open her eyes. He had no idea what was happening here or what had snapped in Roger's brain, but he knew FEMA and the National Guard weren't going to show up anytime soon to save them from this secondary catastrophe. How could they survive an apocalypse only to be murdered by a crazed lunatic in their backyard?

"Help me, Jeff," Roger instructed. "The gods...the Fates...they demand a sacrifice! We have to throw her into the volcano."

Two large strides and Jeff had his hands on Roger Gleason. He easily wrestled him to the ground, as Roger's beleaguered breathing grew hoarse, gasping in his efforts. The fight went out of him quickly and Jeff almost felt sorry for him.

Almost.

Jeff punched him hard across the face, knocking him completely out.

Then he lunged to Amy, who cried out. "It's okay, baby. It's okay."

He freed her arms and pulled her into his own, trying to

calm his laboring heart. She slumped into him and began to cry softly. Jeff looked up at the grey sky and realized ash was no longer falling. Amy was looking at the sky as well. She pointed gingerly and her voice cracked as she spoke: "Bird."

"What?" he followed her gaze.

High up, the silhouette of a bird floated just below the clouds. *A bird*, Jeff wondered silently.

"There's hope," Amy said.

In her eyes, Jeff could see the future.

An Afterword to this story is on page 242.

7

THE INCOMPARABLE
ANGIE WILLIAMS

by
Lynette White

Angie Williams, Mayor of Kinonville, stood on the highest hill north of town overlooking what was left of her city. Her long brown hair, usually meticulously prepared, was carelessly tied back with a simple hair tie. The perfectly tailored business suits she was usually seen in were replaced with jeans and T-shirts. Her scraped up hands and arms were tightly wrapped around her tiny frame as she wept openly for those she couldn't save.

A river of lava was eating up her life as it flowed through her town. Everyone knew they lived at the base of a sleeping volcano but it showed no sign of waking up until the massive earthquake four days ago. The radio reported the earthquake measured 8.0. What was not destroyed in the quake was finished off when the mountain ripped open.

Kinonville was home to 10,000 people but they only found 500 survivors. Roughly a thousand managed to escape between the quake and the volcano coming to life. No one knew if those who fled were safe somewhere or dead from the aftershocks.

Angie was among those who went from house to house searching for survivors until it became too dangerous to stay in the city. She personally saved over 100 men, women, and children but still considered herself a failure because she couldn't do more.

Two days and a night passed before her body finally refused to take another step. David Evans, the Fire Chief, threatened to get one of the doctors to sedate her if she did not lie down and get some sleep. She had no strength left to argue with him and collapsed on a cot. Yesterday morning she woke up refreshed and has only slept five hours since.

The survivors behind her were creating makeshift shelters out of tents and whatever materials they could salvage. Ten volunteers made one more trip to town yesterday to salvage what supplies they could before Kinonville disappeared.

This morning she took a survey of the supplies. She determined there was enough food and medicine for about two weeks. Meaning, a decision would have to be made soon. Do they stay and hope for a rescue or take the survivors and try to find the rest of humanity?

The reports on the radio were bleak before the signal went dead the morning after the quake. Apparently the entire earth's crust suddenly decided to realign itself. Billions of people were dead. The morning after the quake, communication around the world ceased. The Kinonville survivors feared they were on their own until one man salvaged his Ham radio. Late last night he reached the US Army, or what was left of it. He was told it might be weeks before any help reached them.

"Angie," a cautious voice addressed her.

She cringed at the sound of her ex-husband's voice. He should have been fifty miles away with the woman he left her for. He was the last thing she could deal with right now.

She wiped away the tears and slowly turned around. "What are you doing here, Alan?"

He honestly looked hurt but she could care less. She could never inflict enough pain on him to equal the pain he caused her.

"I came to make sure you were alright and get some help. Kingston was wiped out by the quake and only a handful of us got out alive. We were hoping…" He stopped and looked at the ground.

She scanned him from head to foot. His black hair was longer, nearly reaching his shoulders. His body was still strong and solid so she assumed he was still in construction. His green eyes didn't dance like they used too and stress lines were developing around his eyes and mouth. The last time she saw him was three years ago in divorce court but he still made her heart skip a beat.

"You were hoping for what?" She pressed tersely.

"Angie please, we salvaged what vehicles we could and came here because both of our doctors are dead. I have a lot of injured people and I don't want you to punish them because of what I did to you." He pleaded.

Now she was angry. "Do you honestly think I would do that just because I hate you?" She snapped and pushed past him. "You are still a jerk."

She retuned to camp with him right on her heels to find it in chaos. Some stranger was standing in the center of camp barking orders. She turned toward Alan and pointed in the direction of the stranger.

"Who is that?" she demanded.

Alan flinched. "Umm…that is Sheriff Jake Winters."

"Your sheriff?" She repeated and spun back around. "Well, your sheriff needs to learn some manners!"

The people of Kinonville stopped what they were doing. Mayor Williams stormed through camp as if she were her own force of nature. She was heading straight for the young sheriff.

"You! Move those supplies over there!" Jake yelled.

"Don't touch a thing, Cory!" She countered and Cory froze.

"Excuse me, I am Sheriff Jake Winters and if these people are going to survive there must be some order here," he argued.

"I don't care if you are Sheriff Buford Pusser! You will not come in here and start pushing people around like we are a bunch of stupid sheep," she shot back.

The sheriff squared up with Angie. He was younger, a good foot taller and easily twice her size. His uniform was filthy and his brown hair was equally coated with dirt. He obviously did his part to rescue the handful of survivors, but that did not give him just cause to start taking things over. He crossed his arms and tensed up for a fight. His jaw quivered in rage as his eyes moved over Angie from the top of her head to the filthy white tennis shoes on her feet. Her arms were also crossed and she was not the least bit intimidated by the bigger man.

"And who are you to question my authority?"

"I am Mayor Angie Williams. This hill is part of my city and therefore my jurisdiction. This isn't even your county so I am the authority here, not you!"

She stopped and looked into the crowd. Dan Davis, the Police Chief, was making his way through the crowd. He was a career officer and spent the last ten years of his twenty-two on the force as the chief.

"I have my Police Chief here, Sheriff Winters, and he is doing a fine job keeping things in order. Now you are more then welcome to assist Chief Davis. Or you can go right back over the hill you came over. Do I make myself clear?"

Dan finally reached them and looked from one to the other. It appeared neither one of them were about to give an inch. He sighed and addressed his fellow officer first.

"Jake, I see you have met our esteemed Mayor Angie Williams. She may be little but she is a package of dynamite."

Alan chuckled and she glared at him. He cleared his throat and looked at the ground. This was not the time to test her.

The young sheriff dropped his arms as he switched his focus to his collogue. "Chief Davis, it is good to see you again. I apologize, I didn't know you were here. I was trying to organize the civilians."

66

His eyes moved back to Angie. "My apologies, Mayor Williams. I am afraid it has been a long four days and I guess I let the stress of the situation get the better of me," he apologized.

She relaxed her pose as well and nodded in return. "Apology accepted. I will turn you over to Chief Davis while I tend to your people." She stated and motioned for Alan to take her to them.

Dan chuckled as Angie and Alan walked off. "I am doing what I can, but I will take any help I can get."

Jake just shook his head. "Whew. So that is Alan's ex-wife, huh? No wonder he took off with Barb. Not that it did him any good."

Dan looked at him with a raised eyebrow. "Meaning?"

Jake laughed. "Barb took off on him over a year ago because she got tired of a crowded relationship. Seems he never quite got over Angie."

Dan laughed with him. "Huh, bet Angie doesn't know that. Fact is, she never got over him either. Who knows, the next few days could change everything for those two."

He pointed into the heart of the camp. "Come on, I'll show you around."

Two days later Angie and Alan were tending to the wounded when they heard the distinctive sound of chopper blades. They rushed out to the clearing where a crowd was gathering. The crowd cheered as the large military chopper came over the hills from the south and flew over what used to be Kinonville.

As the pilot circled over the camp the crowd cleared an area for him to land. Once it touched the ground one man dressed in a US Army uniform jumped out. As he moved toward the crowd, it was obvious he was looking for someone in charge.

Chief Davis joined Angie and Alan as they made their way through the crowd. Angie noted the silver leaf on the man's uniform.

She extended a hand as they came together. "Lieutenant Colonel, I am Mayor Angie Williams and this is Alan Brighton."

She nodded at Dan. "This is Chief Dan Davis. We were told we wouldn't see anyone for weeks."

The Lieutenant Colonel shook Angie's hand first. "Mayor Williams, Chief Davis, I am Lieutenant Colonel Jack Mcquire. We reconsider after that radio message and made you a priority. How many do you have here?"

"We have a total of 615 but we don't have a lot of supplies left. Is there anywhere you can help us get to?" Angie asked.

The Lieutenant shook his head. "Not quickly. The only way to get these people out of here is to airlift them. The safest area is nearly 300 miles away, but there is a lot of devastation between here and there."

"Is that possible?" Alan pressed.

"It is…but it will take awhile. I have to set up accommodations for this many people before I can arrange the evacuation. That takes time. We have evacuation teams spread across the nation, or what used to be the US."

"We might not get to you for another month. How long will your supplies hold out?"

"A month? We only have enough supplies for maybe another week." Angie protested.

"Alright. What I can do is air drop you some food and supplies to get you through. Do you know what you are going to need?"

"Come with me Lieutenant and I will show you what we have," Angie offered.

The Lieutenant scheduled the supply drop in three days and a military radio to come with them to coordinate the evacuations. The wounded, families, and elderly would be evacuated first. It would take a full week before everyone was safely relocated. Angie and Alan would be on the last chopper with the doctor, the radio operator, Dan, and Jake.

Two more weeks came and went before everyone was settled again. Late one evening Angie and Alan slipped away to be alone. Daniel was right, the last few weeks changed them. As they settled in the grass, they saw the tips of two ears pop up over the grass. It was the first wild animal they had seen since the earthquake.

Angie smiled. "Look, a little rabbit. Just goes to show there is hope."

Alan pulled her close. "For him or for us?"

She pulled away. "Careful. I'm still mad at you."

"How many times do I have to tell you I'm sorry?"

Her expression softened. "A few more, but at least I don't want to tear out your heart anymore."

An Afterword to this story is on page 243.

8

A BROTHER'S LOVE

by
Harry Alexiou

"Are mum and dad dead, Petey?" Luke asked quietly, staring down at his shoes.

"Hey, I told you already, don't talk like that…they're gonna be here soon. It's just that the roads are all messed up."

"But they both missed my birthday, Petey, and they never missed it before." Luke wiped away the tears with his sleeve and sniffled loudly.

Pete put his arm around his brother.

"Listen to me, Luke, when this is all over, mum and dad will buy you the best present ever, the one you always wanted."

Luke wiped his eyes some more.

"You mean the remote control Apache helicopter?"

Pete couldn't remember if that was it, but it wasn't hard to play along.

"Yeah, that's the one!"

"You Promise, Petey?"

"Yeah, promise." Pete hugged his brother and held back the tears. He had to stay strong for his brother, the only person alive for whom he cared.

* * *

Pete looked out across the street and to the other two remaining houses. There was no sign of life. He could see down to the low-lying areas of the town where houses, shops, schools, churches and a hospital used to be. Everything except for the three houses in their street had either been devastated by the destructive earthquake or consumed by the tsunami, which had reached inland and battered the untidy debris. He knew they would soon have to venture outside.

"Come on, Luke, help me check the windows for leaks," Pete said as he tried to lift the spirits of his despondent brother. The massive quake had set off volcanoes, which had lain dormant for hundreds of years. The hillside upon which their house stood was close to a technically extinct volcano but it had suddenly burst into life, akin to a fire-breathing dragon woken from its slumber. The ensuing lava flow moved unrelenting down the hillside three weeks ago, continuing through the town, setting fires and melting debris all the way. The stink of noxious sulphur filled the air and some had seeped into the house before Pete had decided to duct tape all the window and door edges.

* * *

The brothers finished checking the windows and descended into the spacious basement.

"Dad knew something would happen one day," said Pete as he poured bottled water into the powdered milk for their breakfast. "Everybody thought he was being overcautious, even crazy, but he was right."

"Is that why he did all this…and kept all this tinned stuff down here?"

"That's right, Luke. He was…he's a smart guy, our dad, and he'll be looking after mum thinking how to get to us." Pete hoped his slip up hadn't registered as he looked across to his brother, now fiddling with the Etch A Sketch.

Pete checked the stock-list hanging on the provisions rack and frowned. Their supplies were being depleted quicker than expected. The stored power from the ash covered PV panels would soon be gone, and the small amount of sunlight fighting through the ash cloud wasn't enough to power anything more than a couple of light bulbs.

"Hey, little guy," Pete said, "we have to start eating less otherwise we'll have to go hunt our own food." He chuckled falsely, but his young brother just continued playing, oblivious to their precarious situation.

* * *

Suddenly, the siblings both turned their heads sharply upward, startled by the loud banging on the front door. Pete put his finger to his lips preventing Luke from breaking their silence. He motioned to his brother to stay put and ascended the wooden staircase avoiding the creaky steps.

"Hello? Anyone in there?" a stranger's voice boomed.

Pete silently manoeuvred himself to the bay window at the front of the house. The windows were far from clear, covered in a thin film of volcanic ash. He squinted at the figure who seemed rooted to the doorstep.

"Hello?" he called again.

The front door shook as the stranger's fist landed again. Pete froze as he suddenly recognised the unexpected visitor. It was Marvin Locke, an older, former school buddy who'd got into a bad crowd five or six years ago and ended up in prison. Pete recalled that he'd recently been locked up for armed robbery and for causing the death of a security guard. His was one of the houses still standing.

Marvin gave up pounding the door and stepped back. He approached the window and cupped his hands to it attempting to see inside. Pete held his breath and wished that he could quieten his rapidly beating heart. The only thing between him and the worst thing to ever happen to their neighbourhood was triple glazing and three feet of air. Marvin backed away and appeared to search for something on the ground, he then disappeared from view.

Pete was dumbstruck as Marvin suddenly reappeared, holding what looked like a large rock. He grabbed the baseball bat stood up by the window and prepared to do battle, muscles taut, pulse racing. Unexpectedly, Marvin turned and looked behind him, distracted by something. He dropped the rock and started running down the incline toward the other two houses.

Pete didn't care why. He sat back and regained his composure, the adrenalin rush slowly subsiding.

"Petey?"

"Luke, what did I say? Stay down there!" Luke retreated watery eyed, faster than a rabbit down a hole.

"Crap," whispered Pete as he immediately regretted his tone.

* * *

Marvin had come back for his girl. She was the reason for his incarceration and his life sentence. If she'd kept her mouth shut they'd never have caught him, and they would have been sunning themselves in paradise. His sentence had been unexpectedly reduced by Mother Nature as the prison walls fell away and the ground beneath him cracked apart. Marvin had heard reports of earthquakes elsewhere before the power outage but had no idea it was this bad. The roads were a mess all over town and that was good news as it meant nobody was coming looking for him. He'd remembered a conversation with Pete Jackson before things went bad and hoped he'd be able to break into the Jacksons house first and get a hold of the hunting rifle kept by Pete's dad. He called out to the man who'd caught his eye from the Jackson's house.

"Hey you!" The startled stranger turned on his heels and re-entered the house. Marvin approached the house coughing as the sulphurous air burnt his throat. He covered his mouth with his jacket but it offered scant relief.

* * *

Pete watched Marvin until he disappeared behind the house. He immediately called down to Luke.

"Hey, Luke, do you think you can draw me that Apache helicopter on the Etch A Sketch?"

"Yeah. Sure, Petey"

"Great. I'll be down in a minute"

Pete grabbed a torch and raced upstairs to the attic. He stood in front of the long steel safe-box, which had been screwed to the floor from inside. The shiny, heavy-duty padlock was inscribed with the words HARDENED STEEL around the thick shackle. He didn't have the key and had searched the house from top to bottom, eventually conceding that his dad must have had the key with him. After the first few days following the devastation Pete had stood in the exact same spot and contemplated smashing the padlock off somehow and taking the gun for protection. He stared down at the box and now, more than ever, wished he could get at the rifle. Marvin would be back and all he had to fight back with was a baseball bat.

"Hey, Petey, where are you? I've finished the helicopter."

Pete cursed the padlock as he rattled it angrily on the hasp. He hurried back down to his brother, preparing himself for cheery conversation.

"Wow! Good job, Luke. Looks like the real thing!"

"Yeah, it does." The young boy responded, all smiles and wide eyed, admiring his masterpiece.

It had been a while since Pete had seen that face and he decided they needed to get out into the open. The only problem was Marvin.

* * *

Pete's thoughts shifted away from Marvin as Luke asked one of those questions only a six year old could ask.

"Petey...do you think if we slept for a whole week then we woke up, everything would be fixed and mum and dad would be back?"

"No, Luke...we just...we need to wait."

Pete wasn't sure how long he could handle the constant barrage of questions without losing it. The claustrophobia was getting to him more and more each day. The last thing he wanted was to fall apart and leave Luke with nobody.

"Tomorrow we're going on an adventure." Pete announced as he held his brother close.

* * *

Pete woke up the next morning, stressed by a fitful nights rest, and sat on the edge of the camp bed. He lingered a while and watched Luke sleeping, so peaceful, so ignorant of the facts of their predicament. He envied his young brother as he quietly climbed the stairs and entered the front room of the house. Pete looked outside to the street, still bathed in semi darkness, the ash-cloud sunrise. It was odd to look out and not see a tree, a bird or any living thing. The view of the other two houses, mangled car wrecks, and solidified rivers of lava, was their new landscape and he hated it. Tears rolled down his cheeks in a rare display of emotion as he stared out, watery eyed, at their Armageddon.

The sounds emanating from the basement shook Pete back to reality as he wiped his face dry and prepared, once more, to be the rock in his brother's life.

"Morning, Luke!" called Pete not waiting for a response. "Let's have breakfast and grab the gas masks. We're going out today!"

"Aaaww, do we have to? What if mum and dad come back and we're not here?"

"We won't be long." Pete responded as he descended to the basement.

"Can we leave a note on the door, just in case?"

"Great idea, bro." Pete enthused, "Why don't *you* write it for them?"

Luke beamed and excitedly pulled a sheet of paper from his art folder choosing a thick blue crayon to write his message. The slight earth tremor went unnoticed.

* * *

They stood on the doorstep with gas masks firmly fitted. As Pete watched his brother pinning the message to the door, he had one eye on the house opposite. The baseball bat hung at his side. *Where was Marvin?*

"Hey, Pete!"

Pete's heart sank as he turned to face Marvin, who'd seemingly appeared from nowhere.

"Long time no see," offered the convict.

77

"Yeah…it's been a while," Pete replied. His stomach knotted as he noticed bloodstains on Marvin's clothing.

"Came 'round banging the door yesterday. Guess you were out." Marvin coughed repeatedly. "Don't suppose you got a spare mask for an old friend, Pete?"

Pete ushered Luke behind him and tightened his grip on the bat.

"'Fraid not Marv'. Just what you see." Pete felt the ground tremble beneath his feet but his focus was elsewhere.

"Huh…okay," Marvin responded. "Where're the folks?"

"Mum and dad are coming back soon, we left a note for them," offered Luke as he peeked out from his brothers shadow. Another tremor, this time it registered with the trio as Marvin began laughing at the youngster's comment.

"Coming back? You gotta be kidding. They're probably dead already. Look around you, kid."

Luke started crying as the cutting remarks eroded his long held belief.

Pete couldn't keep it in as he suddenly launched forward with the bat and hit home with terrific force leaving Marvin moaning on the driveway. Another sudden tremor threw them all to the ground and it continued as the ground heaved. Pete grabbed Luke's hand, just in time as a major fissure opened up and left Marvin dangling into the abyss. The sorry sight of a man clinging on to life, the fear in his eyes, his plea for help, was hard to ignore but Pete did just that. He shielded his brother as Marvin disappeared from view. The quake continued for twenty seconds more, then silence.

"Are you hurt, Luke?"

"I'm scared, Petey," sobbed the youngster.

Pete held his brother close reassuringly, checking for injuries.

"Let's go back inside," Pete said.

Luke stopped suddenly and looked to his brother. "What's that noise?"

Pete stopped dead in his tracks and turned his head, listening.

"Helicopter!" screamed Pete recognising the unmistakable *thump-thump* of the rotor blades.

"Is it Apache, Petey?" the excited youngster shouted.

"Much better than that, Luke...much better," Pete replied as he waved his arms skyward.

An Afterword to this story is on page 244.

MERCY KILLING

by
Randall Lemon

"Well, thank God, you're alive."

I opened my eyes. My eyelids felt like they were covered with the grit from sandpaper. When I began to focus, all I saw was a large black blob looming over me. It didn't seem to be bright out but my eyes must have been closed quite awhile and my vision was still blurred.

"So, is anything broken?"

I recognized the voice now. It was my older brother, Hank. I experimentally tried to move. Everything hurt, but all the parts seemed to move okay. I tried to speak to tell Hank that I thought I was okay. But all that came out was a raspy sound.

"Here, take a small sip of this."

I felt something pushed to my lips and some kind of sweet liquid trickled over my parched lips and down my throat. He didn't give me much.

"Wouldn't want you to have survived the fires, just to

choke to death on some pear juice would I?"

Nothing Hank said made sense. "Fires, what fires?" It still didn't sound like me talking, but at least what came out sounded like words. I felt Hank's arm snake around me and pull me roughly up to a sitting position. My eyes were working better now that I wasn't looking straight up and I could see that I was sitting in the middle of a blackened mess. Half burnt timbers and crumbled masonry lay all around.

"Believe it or not, it's a good thing you were buried in all those bricks, or you might have been roasted alive."

I focused on Hank and saw piles of junk lying all around him. "What's all that stuff?" I pointed feebly at the piles.

"Oh, that's what I was able to scrounge from our house and the ones right around us. I've got canned goods in this pile, weapons and ammo in that pile, tools over there, and just some other stuff I thought might be useful in the last one."

"How long did it take you to get all that stuff? And what happened here?"

Hank looked at me with the usual disgusted look he gave me. We've never been very close and to tell the truth I've never really liked him. He was always the big-time athlete and I was always the gamer nerd. He'd been picking on me for as long as I can remember. From my point of view, he was always rotten. When we were little kids, he used to find nests and take the baby birds out of them to show me. Then he would toss them up into the air just to watch them splay on the cement when they couldn't fly. He used to take lighter fluid and matches and set fire to ant holes just to watch them burn. But I guess I should be grateful to him now, he had saved me.

"I've been digging through the wreckage of the fires for almost two days when I realized I'd never be able to carry all this stuff by myself, so I took a chance and looked for you figuring you'd at least be good to help carry things. I figure I'll carry the weapons and ammo and you can carry everything else. That's why I wanted to make sure you didn't have any broken bones. If you had, I figured I'd have to put you out of your misery. I doubt if we'll find any doctors around. Most of the houses in our neighborhood were destroyed by the lava or fires started by the hot ash that spewed into the air. But I found these binoculars, and I can see a couple houses on the far south side near what used to be 45th Street that look to still be standing. I thought we'd head that way first."

"Hank, I'm really hungry, man. You say I've been buried under those bricks for almost two days? Why'd you wait so long to get me out? I need to eat and drink before we go anywhere."

Hank gave me that *do what I say or I'll beat your butt* look of his. "You'll eat and drink when I'm ready to eat and drink Freddie. Remember, I'm the one that found this stuff, so I'm the boss. Now start cramming stuff into that backpack and anything you can't fit, we'll put into bags and hang them from your neck. Now, Vamoose!"

I could see Hank was in an ugly mood and since he had the weapons and I didn't, I figured it was best to listen to him. We started picking our way through the rubble. Every now and then Hank would stop at a rubble pile to pick through it and then shove something into one of my bags. Once he came up with some kind of pistol that I identified as a Desert Eagle from playing role playing games. He kept that himself.

I really needed a drink but Hank just kept shoving me along. Suddenly I heard a groan from off to the left. I told Hank and we went over that way. There was an old man trapped under some rubble. He looked so glad when he saw us. Hank walked over to him and asked how he was.

"Oh, I'm fine, fine now that you boys are here. Dig me out, would you?"

Hank looked down at him as I started putting down bags. "You got any guns, ammo, food, or anything else?"

"How would I know? I've been buried here since the wall that used to hold the fireplace crumbled all over me. Now, be a good kid and dig me out and we'll see what we can find."

Hank looked at me and said, "Who told you to put the bags down?" Then he turned back to the man. "I've got a better idea." With that he pulled out the pistol, flipped off the safety and shot the man right in the head. Blood splattered in all directions. "Now I'll look and see what I can find, and I don't have to waste time digging you out."

I couldn't believe what I'd seen. Hank had always been a jerk but... "Hank you killed that man, he was a complete stranger, why?"

"Number one, he wasn't a stranger, I recognized him right away. He was the librarian at my high school. One time he kicked me out and I got my library privileges suspended because he said I was bullying some kids around. Guess he won't be kickin' anyone out of any library anymore. Anyway, he was old. I wasn't about to babysit some old geezer. Now shut up and watch the stuff while I look for anything useful."

"But Hank, you can't just kill people, it's not right."

"Listen to me you snot-nosed little punk, I've got the gun so that makes whatever I do right. The only reason you're here is because I don't have a mule, so you'd better hope I don't come across one. If I do, you'll find out how right this gun makes me!" Spittle shot from his mouth as he yelled at me.

I was in a panic. I could see the madness in Hank's eyes. I had always suspected he was close to being psychotic, now I could see he had crossed over. I realized being brothers meant nothing. My life meant nothing and I knew that sooner or later I'd wind up like that librarian.

A half hour later we were on the go again. Suddenly Hank just stopped and stared off to the right. Looking that way I saw some movement. "Look, Hank, dogs!"

"Those aren't dogs you idiot, they're coyotes. I'd seen them in our neighborhood but only at night. Now that people are way scarcer, they're out and about in daylight too."

"What do you think they're doing, Hank?"

"The same thing we are, you stupid turd, they're scavenging food. Guess we'd better camp, we'll get to those standing buildings tomorrow. We're going to have to take turns watching so those coyotes don't come in on us while we're asleep. We'll build a fire. After we eat, you sleep. I'll wake you up in a few hours. Then you can build the fire up and watch while I sleep."

"When do you think people will show up to help? Shouldn't there be firemen and police or National Guard or somebody?"

Hank scanned the horizon, "Hopefully not for a long time. I figure the earthquake that started all this must've been pretty widespread. Maybe the whole country had volcanoes forced to the surface and exploded. Before everything went to hell, I heard something about an earthquake setting off a tidal wave that was supposed to drown the entire West Coast, so maybe they've got way more to worry about than just our little neighborhood. So all you have to worry about is doing what I say, and I say let's get ready to set up a camp."

"Okay, but you'll need to show me how to use one of the guns."

"Like hell! I'm not giving you a gun. If you see or hear something, wake me up."

"But how am I going to keep the fire going?"

"Geez, you're stupid. No wonder Mom and Dad couldn't stand you!"

"That's right!" I hadn't even thought about them. I couldn't believe it. "Wait, what happened to Mom? She was in the house with us making dinner. And Dad, he must be looking for us."

"Listen! Let me make the facts of our new life clear to you. I found Mom before I found you, when I was looking for food in what was left of our house. She's dead, Freddie. Burned to death."

He sounded completely passionless as he told me our Mother was dead, just like it was any old fact, like, "That wall is red." I started to cry and his hand snaked out and slapped me hard.

"No crying! There's nothing we can do about it. She's

85

dead and Dad probably is too."

"But he wasn't even at home. He was in the city or heading back for dinner. He must be okay!"

"Okay," said Hank, "pick everything up and follow me." He led me over to an area that looked like freshly laid black tar. It was still steaming in places. "You see this, numbskull? This is what's left of one of the rivers of lava that came pouring down the side of that volcano which popped up during the earthquake. Dad is not coming home because his car is probably buried under one of these rivers. Nobody's comin' back. They're all dead or digging themselves out of fallen buildings just like I did. Now grab some hunks of that lava rock, but be careful to get some of the cooler ones. We'll use them to create a circle in which to build our campfire. Keep your eyes opened for anything that will burn on our way back to where we want to make camp."

Hank found a place he thought would make a good campsite and he started spreading the rocks in a circle. "Put my stuff down and go find some of that wood we spotted on the way back and hurry it up. I'll dig us out something to eat."

I practically broke my back trying to bring back enough wood to make Hank happy enough to not hit me and hoping I would get enough to eat. I couldn't keep going on like this. Hank didn't care if Mom and Dad were dead. He'd killed a trapped old man for yelling at him in the library and now I was at his mercy. He didn't like me and I had the feeling that once the food and water got scarce, he'd drop me like a bad habit. I didn't know what to do. He wasn't about to give me a weapon. He already had Dad's hunting rifle, a bowie knife and a machete that I knew of, as well as that Desert Eagle .44 revolver. The fact that he wouldn't even allow me to touch one made me uneasy about my future. But what could I do about it? And what if we ran into more helpless people? What would he do to them?

When I dropped the wood down near the campfire site instead of looking satisfied, he started yelling at me again. "Omigod, you retard! What am I going to do with all these big boards? We're making a campfire not a bonfire!" He reached into the bag that had the tools in it and pulled out what looked like a Boy Scout hatchet. Go over there and chop that wood into pieces no longer than your arm. You're not getting anything to eat until you get it done."

I dragged the wood over to where he had indicated and started chopping and breaking it down to pieces about 18' in length. Hank sat there eating from a can and watched me till he got bored. It started to get dark and Hank finally let me get something to eat. He gave me a can of whole kernel corn while I notice he had eaten a can of ravioli and a can of beef stew. He told me to go to sleep and tossed me an old, torn blanket. I was so tired, I didn't feel like arguing.

Before I knew it he was shaking me. "Throw some wood on the fire and watch till morning. Once the sun comes up, build the fire up again and wake me. Instead of using the flimsy blanket he had given me, he zipped himself up in a big canvas and fleece sleeping bag. I went over to the boards to get some to build up the fire. I heard something moving around and froze. I was petrified. "Should I wake Hank? Maybe it was someone who was hurt or maybe it was a pack of coyotes." Now I saw something move out of the corner of my eye and found myself staring at the flank of a white-tailed deer. It seemed that the coyotes weren't the only wildlife returning to what used to be our suburban neighborhood. I left the deer alone and it finally wandered away. The fire was burning low and I returned to my woodpile. As I crouched down to pick up the wood, I saw it there: the answer to all my problems, that Boy Scout hatchet. Hank was all zipped up in that sleeping bag and it would be hard for him to move or to defend himself.

All I had to do was pick up the ax, creep over to him and pull a *Lizzie Borden*. It was him or me. I had killed enough imaginary people and monsters in the games I played. We always used to say that *sleep plus one melee round equaled death.* How hard could it be? I would just keep hitting him until his head looked like red jelly. Then I would have the food and weapons and maybe I could find some nice people and help them and they would call me a hero and introduce me to their pretty daughter. That would be cool! The hero always gets the princess. He may have been my brother, but he was a bad person. I remembered something from the story of Cain and Abel in the Bible. Cain had killed his brother and when someone asked where Abel was, Cain responded, "Am I my brother's keeper?" I needed to kill Hank in order to protect the princess and her family and any other innocent people we might run into, and to protect myself. I needed to be the keeper for all my brothers and sisters of the earth. I would be doing the world a favor by putting this bully down once and for all.

I crept over next to Hank and raised my hatchet. Hank's eyes flew open and he smiled.

"Boom."

Incongruously, I noticed a smoldering hole in Hank's nice sleeping bag. I fell to my knees and the hatchet dropped from my quickly numbing fingers. "So that's what the Desert Eagle sounds like close up!" I looked down and my thin shirt was sticky and wet.

I started to fall backward over my heels and I heard Hank say, "I knew I couldn't trust you, Freddie, you and those stupid games you used to play all the time. That was fantasy, Freddy, and this is reality. What really pisses me off is that now I'm going to have to carry all this stuff myself until I find someone else to use. You are such an idiot."

An Afterword to this story is on page 245.

10

THE LAST DAWN

by
Christian W. Freed

Every culture has myths about the end of the world. The apocalypse. Armageddon. Ragnarok. Judgment Day. Very few have any true idea what reality might offer. We'd grown up hearing our elders talking about how California would fall into the ocean. My favorite was the crazy old preacher claiming the Rapture was about to happen on this date at this time. He even had the nerve to go back on television after he was wrong and say he got the date confused. No one really knows what happened to him after that. Not that any of it mattered. We figure most of the world died shortly after.

It took a while before folks were able to figure out what really happened. Increased solar flares triggered a violent reaction in the Earth's core, causing ever volcano to simultaneously erupt. Earthquakes ripped the land apart. The skies darkened with ash. Most of the streams and lakes were polluted with sulfur. Oceans rushed across the globe like avenging angels. Whole islands were submerged and lost forever. Our world changed that day.

How many millions, possibly billions, died in those first few months we'll never find out but we guessed it was most of the population. That was thirty-five years ago. I'm an old man now; beaten and broken. I never had the life my parents hoped. Instead I took to guarding what was left of my town from marauders and mutants.

Every day we patrolled the edges of the lava fields surrounding Harbor on three sides. (The town used to be named something else, no one rightly remembers, but Harbor fit better.) We became a refuge for lost souls and displaced survivors. Things went well for a while but then folks stopped coming. Not that it mattered much. Harbor was beyond capacity, forcing the gatherers to range farther and farther away from the safety of our walls just to find food and water.

"Well, look at that!" Brady exclaimed suddenly, disturbing me from my thoughts.

I looked to where he was pointing and we both hurried over. Three small flowers had bloomed. White petals sprayed out in a wide circle around a perfect golden orange center. Flowers!

"I'll be," I said. "I don't recall the last time I saw flowers in the wild."

Brady, hardly twenty years old, never knew the old world. The flowers represented unlimited possibilities for the future as well as the casual reminder of what the past was. "They're beautiful."

"I guess they are," I told him. "Maybe the world is changing again."

"Do you think there's more?"

I shrugged, not wanting to get my hopes up. Disappointment ruled Harbor for too many years and I didn't want to be the one responsible for invoking more.

"What are you two Marys looking at?"

I cringed at the voice. Brady's face hardened and he spun to watch William march up the slope. The town bully, William, had about as much compassion as a dead fly.

"What do you want? Your job is down at the mill," I told him, not wanting the inevitable confrontation.

William was a brute of a man, built like a brick outhouse and just as mean. His red hair, more crimson really, ran down past squared shoulders. He hadn't shaved since puberty and was the meanest man I had ever had the displeasure of meeting. He was also my cousin.

"Don't you think on telling me what to do, our fathers are both dead. That means there's nothing to keep me from beating you to a pulp.

"Easy, William. There's no need for trouble," I said, hoping to present at least the image of authority. "Head on back to town and leave us."

He shoved me to the ground before I knew what was happening and yanked the flowers from the ground in a quick move. "I don't get it. These are worthless!"

William crushed the flowers and tossed them down. Shaking his head, he turned and headed back to Harbor.

Brady struggled to fight back his tears. "Somebody ought to do something about him!"

"Calm down. There isn't any point in getting worked up

over a man like that," I said softly. *Besides, he'll get what's coming to him if there's still a God up there.*

The ruined stalks of long dead pine trees poked up into the grey sky, a visceral reminder of a dead world. The ground was the color of ash. Stone and dirt became one. Those three flowers stood for so much and William casually destroyed them on a whim. I gathered the remains and took Brady back to Harbor.

William sat at his usual chair at the end of the bar in Fella's Tavern. No one knew where the name stemmed from but after a few decades, it didn't matter. It was the best place to go for a hot meal and what passed for beer. Of course it was the only place in town as well. The common room smelled of smoke and grease. A dozen others were already seated

"Steven! Have you heard the news?" Molly asked, setting down a glass of light brown colored water and a loaf of dark bread.

There was a time I never would have considered drinking the water; once, long ago. "I don't think so," I replied, careful not to mention the flowers.

"Old Stew found horse tracks up on the north ridge," she said cheerfully. "Could be more people."

"More likely a band of marauders," I answered. Mutants didn't ride what they could eat.

Molly pouted. "You shouldn't be so critical. Not everyone can be bad."

Gruff laughter broke out from William's end of the bar. His usual group of thugs had gathered to listen to him recount his handling of the earlier encounter by the edge of the lava fields. I grew angry, but not enough to make a scene. My cousin was many things; fool chief among them. He'd tried to take over Harbor once but the townsfolk stood up and forced him back down. After that he turned to petty crimes, a little thievery, and the occasional fistfight. Nothing too serious but enough to have some of the elders call for his banishment.

I'd stepped up and convinced them not to throw William out into the world. He was my cousin after all and sometimes blood trumped good judgment. He found out about my involvement and has hated me ever since.

"There he is!" William bellowed and I closed my eyes. "My big bad cousin sitting by his lonesome. Where is everyone? Don't you have any friends?"

"You leave off, William! I'll not have a fight in the common room," Molly scolded.

The laughter doubled. "Ah, never could do your own dirty work. Now you need a woman to stand up for you. Go home, little boy. Let men do their thing."

Molly took a step forward before I managed to stop her. The look in my eye told her enough. I rose slowly. Adrenaline amped me up. I didn't like to fight, hardly saw the point in it, but enough was enough. William needed to be reminded of his station in life.

"That's enough, William. You talk too much," I said.

His chair scraping back screeched throughout the room, stopping all conversation. He was much larger than me, but my father instilled the sense that size was the least important factor in a fight. I prayed he was right.

William looked me dead in the eye. "What are you going

to do about it?"

I opened my mouth but the door opening loudly behind me interrupted up. Close to twenty men crowded into the tavern, led by a very angry Brady. The youth pointed at William and his group closed in. More confident in large numbers, William's followers backed off. Especially upon seeing the weapons brandished by the angry crowd.

"Brady, what's the meaning of this?" I demanded.

Brady looked at me with a face caught between rage and sadness. "He's a bad person, Steven. William's gone and killed the first sign of life we've had in the outside world since I've been alive! He's got to pay for that crime."

"There's nothing for it, Steven," Carl, the candle maker said. "The whole town is plain tired of William and his bullying. It's past time we stood up to it and put him back in his place."

Confused, I asked, "You can't mean—"

"He's got to go, Steven. It's the only way."

Banishment. The word was akin to a death sentence. No one could survive for long outside of our little valley. This punishment wasn't unprecedented. We'd banished several, mostly during the beginning. Newcomers reported on passing skeletons on their way in. Noxious fumes killed our banished within a few miles of safety. Fortunately the city council decided the act was inhumane and a small jail was crafted into the side of the mountain.

Carl laid a hand on my shoulder. "The fumes have to be gone by now. It's been almost four decades since the Event. He'll be fine if he can make it to another village."

"Banish me for what?" William demanded angrily.

Old Stew stared him down. "Murder."

Even William appeared taken back as hushed silence gripped us all. "I haven't killed no one!"

"Perhaps not, but it's murder nonetheless. Brady told us about the flowers, the very first flowers any of us has seen since the Event. This is unforgivable."

William spit. "For flowers? Not a soul in this village cares about flowers, old man."

"It's new life!" Molly all but screamed. "You didn't just kill a handful of flowers, William. You killed hope that the future might be getting better."

"Take him into custody," Stew ordered.

Men surged forward to flexi-cuff William's hands behind his back and shove him out of the tavern. No one else dared move, fearful of what might come next.

"Is this it?" I asked. "This is what we've become? A frightened village living in a police state?"

Old Stew shook his head. "Police state? When have we ever been less than just? Every last person in Harbor gives one hundred percent to make life better. All it takes is one bad seed to contaminate the garden. Look, I know he's your cousin, but we can't let that stop justice."

"I don't see justice here, Stew, only sheep," I replied and went home.

Dawn came much too quickly. The banished were always sent away at dawn under the philosophy that they stood a better chance of living that way. For myself I didn't know. I didn't want to know. The only truth I saw was that my one remaining family member was being sent away. At least Stew and the council gave me the option of having a few moments alone.

William stood, legs shoulder width apart, and hate in his heart. "You'd best leave me, *cousin*. I ain't in a generous mood."

"I don't know what to say," I told him. "Why do you always have to meddle?"

He snorted. "I was made like this! Go ask the one who made me. Now bug off!"

Perhaps the council was right. Perhaps William was the bad seed, irredeemable and callous as a hard winter. I watched my cousin take those first fateful steps into the path between lava fields. His walk seemed angry and hateful. William might be leaving us, banished for life, but I couldn't shake the feeling that I was going to be seeing him again real soon.

Sometime later, close to sundown, a great commotion broke out in Harbor. Everyone that could flocked to the town square to find out what it was. Three score of men and women on horseback reigned in, each wearing a camouflaged uniform complete with the ragged patch of the former United States flag.

"What's the name of this town?" their leader asked.

I stepped forward. "Harbor. Who are you?"

He grinned and removed his cap. "Captain Larry Archibald of the Third Reconstituted Cavalry Regiment, United States Army."

"We thought the world had ended with the *event*," Carl said.

"Quite nearly," CPT Archibald answered. "It took us forever to start the reconstruction process but there's a new government and an army. We've got hundreds of elements out trying to find survivors just like you."

"So it's over," Molly whispered.

Archibald nodded.

"What about flowers?" Brady asked excitedly. "Are there flowers?"

"Flowers, trees, fresh fruits and vegetables and a fair amount of drinking water. People of Harbor, it is my pleasure to invite you to join the new United States of America."

The townsfolk cheered. It was finally over.

Ah William, I lamented, looking back towards the edge of town and the lonely path of banishment, *you couldn't have kept your mouth shut for one more day?*

An Afterword to this story is on page 246.

11

DRAGONSHIP

by
H.M. Schuldt

Is it the same ship from the day before? Along with everyone else in Elton's house of eighty-two people, I wondered why the ship in the distance wouldn't sail closer to our island. We were stuck on a new cliff between the Neuse River and the Tar River, surrounded by the Atlantic Ocean. After the great earthquake hit North Carolina and the rest of the world in the summer of 2025, most of Nash County buckled and sank. But a certain crack set in, pushing part of our street up high enough to escape a new volcano.

I hoped the far off ship was headed our way to save us. We all did. I never gave up the possibility that we were next on the captain's list for his subsequent rescue. It wasn't until later when I learned why the captain kept his distance from our harbor. He had seen several of the houses in my neighborhood slide down into the ocean, covered by crumbling limestone and sandstone bluffs. He saw hot magma pour into the ocean, blocking his path to reach us. Our neighborhood island was unstable and we had to find a way out.

Tension grew among two hundred people on Nash Island where, one by one, more houses slid into a mudflow of pyroclastic material, rocky debris, and water. In the beginning, Lily and I were at Elton's house of *eighty-two people* until Lily asked me, "Elton slurs all the time, doesn't he?" I knew we couldn't live with his type. People who jaunted about as a liar and a thief were no company for Lily and me. He talked and he talked. He talked about making a longboat for our big escape. The *Dragonship* he called it, but at the rate he was going, it seemed as if the boat would never get started.

"What's your favorite season?" I asked young Lily.

"I don't know, Miss Margaret. I like all of them."

Lily and I had no family on the island. I couldn't leave her by herself with her own sense of adventure. She had found a golden seahorse and kept it with her at all times. "Lily, I can't stand being around Elton. We shouldn't stay here anymore. Elton's lost his mind. He's more concerned about building a dragon head for himself than making sure we get off the island."

The young girl's penetrating eyes gave me a look of uncertainty. Yet her little figure, strong with poise and posture, was very dignified. "Elton won't let us go to another house. He acts like we're his pets. You heard him. He even calls me his *pet*."

"Well, we're not pets. Not even. He treats us like we are his property because he can't think straight. He owns this big house, but he doesn't own us, Lily. You're coming with me."

"Where are we going?"

"Away from Elton. Samson started making a longboat. Let's ask Samson if we can sail out with him."

It was quite dark that night when we set out to speak to Samson and learn more about his construction project, the *White Pelican*. I greeted Samson at the door. "Hi. I'm Margaret."

Lily and I met Samson the longboat builder that night at Roger's house. There he was, strong and heavenly. Everything about his echelon in woodworking was by far superior. "The past is gone. We do things differently than Elton. I'm Samson. I'll let you stay here if you follow directions. You both have to work everyday. You can start by making oars, and we'll give you a meal once a day from Norma the cook." Young Lily and I moved into what was called *Roger's House*. Only two other houses held more people than his, *Elton's House* and *Ferrell's House*. The rooms at Roger's were like small apartments and the kitchen became our cafeteria.

On the first day after the ash cleared the air, our leader Roger set out to catch rainwater. He returned and frequently took a head count of fifty-five. Every bucket was set out to collect as much drinking water as possible. When the rain came down three days in a row, we had a large celebration. Roger said our celebration would cause the rain to keep coming down for another three days. *Wait. Our celebration could do what? Heavy rainfall can cause another mudslide.*

"How's that?" Lily asked me, much too inquisitively.

"I don't know, Lily. Roger has a loose screw in his head just like Elton. Whatever you do, don't ever wander off alone with Roger. Always check in with me. Promise?"

"I promise," Lily smiled, possessing fine qualities of courage and honor.

Two days after the rain stopped, Roger went into another fit of rage. Lily gave me an innocent look so I gave her the duty of being a Ship Lookout for the rescue crew to return and it was a special place where she could play. Roger's anxiety grew worse until one day Lily saw a ship far in the east for the third time. His fear suddenly melted when Lily announced the return of the rescue ship, but it sailed right by. Roger's unstable demeanor was noticed. Without grumbling, I focused on making oars for Sam's longboat, the *White Pelican*.

In spite of the cold, Roger and his rugged comrade Samson had explored Nash Island over the next six months. They risked their lives to explore unhinged houses, collecting food for the fifty-five people in our house, including Norma, Lily, and me. It was a long winter trying to keep warm. The men came back telling us stories about houses that had slid down the cliff from the movement of mud just moments after they escaped with as much food as they could carry.

Our house had enough food, but Elton from the house of *eighty people* returned to demand that Norma give up part of our food.

"Well, well, what you got there?" Elton eyed Lily's golden seahorse.

"Leave her alone, Elton," Roger said.

Pressure grew between Elton and Roger until Elton threw the first punch. Samson pulled Elton off of Roger. I smelled alcohol on Elton's breath. His stash of whiskey was enough to keep him fueled each day. It was the third time Elton had barged in at Roger's house to bully Norma about our food. Each time I noticed Elton scowling at me bitterly for leaving. If it wasn't for brawny Samson, Roger might not have had a chance to keep Elton from stealing our food.

After Elton stormed off, Roger had to appoint guards to protect the *White Pelican* from Elton's threat to destroy it. The quiet was suddenly interrupted.

BOOM!

What? Someone has a gun? It shocked everyone at Roger's house. We turned and saw brave Norma standing outside, a strong woman of seventy years who had been working hard to serve the people. "While you foolish men are fighting and causing a scene, the rest of us are missing our chance to get off this island. Little Lily spotted a ship for the fourth time! It finally came back after a long winter. Today's our lucky day!"

Roger ordered our *fifty-five* to head down to the safe cliff. He called it *safe* to calm our nerves, but I knew deep down that it could slide at any moment. Lily stood right on the edge even though we told her to stay back. In the excitement of seeing the ship again, I lost track of Lily until we heard the ten-year old girl scream.

"LILY!" Norma yelled. "HOLD ON!"

I ran after Samson, seeing Lily had slid part way down the cliff. A terrible wind pressed against Lily's thin body and I didn't want a gust to push her off. Lily's hair was blowing as she dangled in a small niche and I could see her little fingers digging into the dirt, methodically looking for security. She turned her head to look out across the ocean and I didn't want her to lose her grip. Samson threw one end of a rope down to her and he told her to grab on. Next to Lily we saw a section of dirt fall into the hot ocean. It sizzled while steam rose up into the cold air.

"LILY!" Norma yelled. "HOLD ON TO THE ROPE! DON'T LET GO!"

Samson called out next. "ON 3, I'M PULLING YOU UP, LILY! YOU HAVE TO HANG ON TO THE ROPE!"

It was extremely stressful. *Is it my fault she was down there? No one told me to watch over her. Hold on, Lily! Keep holding on!*

"1-2-3." Samson managed to use his strength to pull Lily up. He grabbed one little arm and lifted her back up to high ground.

"Lily!" I said, and I gave her a hug. "You were too close to the edge. You have to stay away from the edge, okay?"

"Lily!" Norma scolded. "You stay near Miss Margaret, and don't you run off again."

"Oh, the view was amazing! Did you see it?" Lily said, hardly affected by what had just happened. She smiled. "We need to get to the ship!" She pulled me, all the while in a grand pursuit of waving her arms to flag down the search crew.

At first we were excited to see the ship, but then we saw it sailing away farther and farther just as it had done the summer before. Elton stood watching the ship sail far off in the east. His skin looked unusually yellow and his hands and feet were dry, flaky, and cracked. I tried to keep my distance, but he kept stepping closer to me. He reeked of vomit and stale whiskey. Looking at me with yellow eyes, he said, "Margaret Mae. Now, I know your type. Hold both your hands high and wave. That ship must have a telescope. I bet they'll sail over this way if you smile and show them some skin. Go on. Show them some skin."

"Go back to your house, Elton, before they lock you out. Go back to *eighty* and leave Norma alone." I gazed at his hirsute feet. "Why are you barefoot?"

"My shoes don't fit. Maybe someone at *fifty-five* has a pair that fit. Maybe you can find me a pair. Roger's shoes look like they're about the right size."

"I'm not stealing Roger's shoes. And stop bullying Norma," I said, walking away from his hairy, swollen toes.

It was the last time I ever saw Elton.

One week later, we heard that he began coughing up blood. An acute case of liver failure took him down. His house soon became known as *seventy-nine* and a new leader rose up. They called him Melvin the Knife.

My brave father's advice turned over in my mind ever since the great lava storm hit the Earth. "All seasons must come to an end, Margaret Mae. You'll only find a new beginning if you look for it." *Are you out there somewhere, father? Are you and mother still alive?*

* * *

It was when three houses were left when Lily saw the ship return for the fifth time. She came running inside excited and yelling, "It came back! The ship! The ship!"

"Lily, you can't run off like that!" Norma scolded.

Most of the people in *fifty-five* had given up on the rescue. Even though the crew failed to sail in, Lily never gave up. The people from *fifty-five* stood immobilized when they knew the ship was there, until Roger came in to give them a nudge.

"Go on! Get out there and go wave the red flags!" Roger ordered.

We felt the Earth tremor and it seemed small enough to continue our way outside to see the ship. Lily and I suddenly experienced another jolt. We fell down on the front porch and heard a huge rumbling in the direction of *seventy-nine*. Once the earthquake was over, we saw that Melvin's house was gone and five survivors were swimming in the hot ocean desperately trying to make their way to the cliff.

With only Roger and Ferrell's houses left, our island was getting smaller. We had to find a rescue. And we had to find one quick.

"Lily, stay back from the edge," I ordered.

The young ten-year old girl with wavy blond hair sat down and began to sing Kumbaya.

Melvin the Knife approached me dripping wet. "Forget it. The ship ain't coming for us. I finished building Elton's longboat. We're sailing out. The rescue ship won't come any closer than this. We have to go now, before it's gone. Don't be a fool. We can't stay here. And I don't have room for everyone."

"And so we leave in the…*Dragonship*?" I asked, deciding that his spontaneous plan would be repugnant to Samson. "No. You go. You find a way to come back and find a way to get us off the island. I'm not leaving Lily."

Suddenly Melvin stormed over to Lily and picked her up. Lily screamed and struggled to get away from his incorrigible behavior, but Melvin carried her down to the *Dragonship*. Together they sailed away with four men who survived from *seventy-nine*. The *Dragonship* had been built with forty benches to carry eighty, but it sailed away with only six. They say that the ghost of Elton can be seen on the *Dragonship* whenever it sails at night under the moon.

"She's my lucky charm!" Melvin called out.

Later that night Norma asked me where Lily went. So I told her what happened. "She'll be back, Norma. I know Lily, and she'll find a way to get back here before Roger's house slides."

The next day Norma was outside looking for any sign of the ship. But we saw nothing. She held an ax and began chopping into the side of a large oak tree.

"If you need firewood, Roger has some out back," I said. The situation had taken a toll on everyone, but I hoped for Norma to remain steadfast.

"Nope," Norma gave a strong hurl at the tree. "We still have time."

"But the *White Pelican* is big enough. Norma, we don't need another boat."

"Yes, we do. I can just feel it. We have time."

It seemed ridiculous to think our house could be gone at any moment, but somehow we accepted it. Norma was right to make use of our time. I worked hard all day to make sure fifty-five oars were ready. Several men from *Roger's house* helped Norma in her unwavering determination by chopping down a cedar tree and cutting strips. No one questioned Norma as to who was going to ride in the small cedar strip canoe.

Samson worked the fastest and lasted the longest. "We have enough room on the *White Pelican* and the *Bellamy*. But who knows? Maybe we'll need a canoe."

We felt another aftershock and it made us work harder until our arms felt stiff. I saw hot gases begin to rise up out of the young volcano. Hot magma poured out of Rocky Mount down into the ocean. My only concern was if the hot ocean would cause our longboats to sink. It was a matter of time before the lava ate away at our cliff. Another section of our island began to slide, but our longboats were finally ready. And before sunset, the canoe was finished.

Norma noticed the same rescue ship return in the east. I ran outside with binoculars and spotted a small rowboat. *Lily! Oh-no! Go back! It's too hot! The ocean's too hot right now! Your boat will sink! Go back! Go back!*

It was Lily, smiling and sailing closer to our island in a deadly hot spring. She thought I was waving to her, so she cheerfully waved back. Samson saw the danger she was in, and he heaved Norma's canoe into the hot spring with the help of another strong man who gave him an oar. Samson jumped in by himself and paddled as fast as he could toward Lily.

Sure enough, I felt another rumble and saw Ferrell's house slide down into the flowing river. Only Roger's house was left standing without much of an island surrounding us. Roger and Ferrell began loading people onto the longboats.

"Everyone…in the boat!" Ferrell yelled laconically and Roger rang the bell.

Norma and I counted fifty-three people on twenty-eight benches in the *White Pelican*. Finally we took a seat near the back and set sail. Ferrel's boat followed closely behind with sixty-five people on thirty-three benches. Half way toward the ship, we heard a loud crash. We looked back and saw Roger's house drift and completely sink into a hot spring.

"Miss Margaret!" Lily called out. Samson helped her climb into the *White Pelican*. "I'm so happy to see you again! See? I knew we'd make it."

We noticed Lily's empty rowboat begin to sink.

"Yes," Samson said. "Yes, we did, Lily. But not everyone made it."

"To the rescue ship!" Lily smiled.

The search and rescue crew greeted us with arms wide open. They pulled up the *Dragonship*, the *White Pelican*, Ferrell's longboat, *Bellamy,* and Norma's canoe.

I leaned in toward Lily. "Just like winter has turned to spring, this season in our life has come to an end, Lily. And now we have a new beginning. Promise me you'll never be afraid to start a new season."

"I promise," Lily smiled. Her eyes sparkled ocean blue under the moon. "Miss Margaret? Hey, guess what? I decided that I do have a favorite season."

"And which one is it?"

"Springtime."

"Sounds like a good name for Norma's canoe."

I sailed away sitting with Lily and Norma. No one talked about what happened that day for a long time. We sat enjoying the peace of sailing into a new horizon. I felt thankful for Samson's dedication to hard work. Without it, we would have become one with the hot magma. Ever since then I have held a deep respect for giving it my best effort, knowing that each day could very well be our last.

Underneath the moonlight in a place so beautiful that it seemed hardly to be of this world, the water glimmered a shiny reflection. The crisp ebony sky and sparkling stars felt closer than ever before. It was quiet and still as though we were gliding through the air like a mother eagle in search of her home. Lily saw something scuttle on the floor in the silver and black night. We saw a grey rabbit sitting up on his haunches eating a wonderful nut.

On we went sailing for a long time, all night over the calm silvery waters. At last we woke up and found ourselves near a gigantic coast of solid ground. It was glorious, towering up before us, its great trees of timeless strength. The first ray of sunshine pierced up in the east and the captain rang a bell.

An Afterword to this story is on page 247.

12

A DEMON UNLEASHED

by
Joyce Shaughnessy

I could smell smoke. Funny how things hit your senses before you wake up. Suddenly my eyes flew open. We'd been warned about the volcano erupting after the earthquake. I sat up and saw devastation all around me, fires smoldering near me. I panicked and ran, looking for something familiar. Why had I fallen asleep? How could I fall asleep when everything around me was leveled? My flattened house was covered in ash and I had nowhere to go.

Then I heard it, a deep, guttural growl. I slowly turned around and standing before me was a German Shepherd, obviously scared just like I was.

"Hi, boy," I uttered, slowly putting my hand out toward him. He turned and ran. *Poor baby. I wonder where he belongs. I wonder where I belong now.*

I turned back toward the neighborhood, determined to find something, anything recognizable and there it stood, a

111

monument of sorts, the only house on my street still standing. Fitting that it was Rhonda's. Nothing ever fell apart for her.

I pushed the lava rocks away from the drive and made my way to the door. It opened at my touch as if it were expecting me. Inside everything was mess, but I could make out the rooms as if it had been on an island, protected from the elements.

I walked into the first floor bedroom and there she lay. Some kind of animal had gotten to her. I turned around and vomited. I'd never seen a human more grotesque or more vulnerable.

Then I heard the sound. It was a baby crying. I ran into the nursery and there he was, Rhonda's baby. *What is his name? Ronald? No. It's Donald. They call him Donnie.*

"Hi, Donnie." I crooned as I picked him up. "Don't worry. I'll take care of you. Aunt Janie's here now, baby boy."

He continued to cry. I changed his diaper and carried him into the kitchen, hoping to find some milk, formula, or something I could feed him. I no longer cared about my growling stomach. Finding nothing, I carried him outside wrapped in a blanket. His skin felt hot and parched. I had to do something for him.

I continued to walk away from the neighborhood, hoping to find someone to help us or something to feed Donnie. That dog was back, but he didn't look scared this time. He started growling again, and I instinctively held the baby against my chest.

"Go away, dog. Go away," I said forcefully. He sat on his haunches, growling. *Maybe he's not a dog at all. Maybe he's a wild wolf. Maybe he killed Rhonda!*

I turned to the left and walked away as fast as I dared. I didn't want him to sense that I was scared of him. I was afraid he'd chase us or even kill the baby. I couldn't, I wouldn't let that happen.

* * *

I must have walked all night long, but it was hard to tell the difference between night and day because the sun was covered up. The whole world seemed to have changed in the blink of an eye. The streets were torn up because of the earthquake, and most of the buildings were leveled either by the earthquake or the volcano. The volcano had erupted lava, which spewed into our neighborhood, but other houses closer to the river had been covered in mud. What difference did it make? As far as I could make out, most of the people were dead.

Donnie cried until he eventually fell asleep. As I walked, I put my fingers in his mouth and he gently sucked on them, but of course, it gave him no nourishment. I was heartbroken because I couldn't find him anything to eat. Finally, I found some water for both of us. I stumbled across a water hose and saw some water dripping from it. I fell on the ground and gave Donnie the first water drip and then gave some to myself. It tasted like the chocolate dripping from my mother's mixing spoon. I had been thirsty for so long that I thought my lips might crack open. Even Donnie smiled at me. I kissed him and inhaled his baby smell.

I had to rest for just a minute. I was so tired, although I knew the danger of falling asleep because it was cold. All Donnie had was a thin little blanket. I told myself that he would be crying soon and would wake me in case I fell asleep. I opened my shirt and lay his little body against mine for warmth. I tried to stay awake, to keep my eyes open, but they finally closed. I don't know how long it had been when I felt myself falling over sideways. I jumped up and pulled Donnie even closer to me.

I can't go to sleep now. I have to go find food somewhere.

The moment I stood up with Donnie, I sensed someone was behind me. I turned around, and right behind me was a boy who looked like he might be about sixteen.

Where have I seen him before? He looks so familiar. Where does he live?

I said to him, "You startled me! I didn't see you standing there. I've been walking forever trying to find other people, anyone alive. Have you seen any other people? Have you found any food or water anywhere? We're both starving and thirsty, especially the baby."

He stood even closer to me, and I must have instinctively stepped back from him because he said, "Are you afraid of me or something? You know, just because other people don't like me doesn't mean I'm a bad person, Janie. In fact, I have some peanut butter sandwiches and Pepsi if you want some."

"How did you know my name?"

The boy leaned closer to me and said, "I know a lot of things about you and little Donnie here." His fingers played with one of Donnie's little curls, and I felt very afraid for Rhonda's baby. I held him more tightly.

Then the boy smiled such a chilling, *ancient* smile that I instantly shuddered. I stepped back again, but not before I smelled a putrid odor like rotting flesh.

"I know, for instance, that if you and Donnie want to come back to my neighborhood with me, I can show you my stash in the garage or what's left of it." He smiled again.

I stuttered, "You mean walk all the way back to *my* neighborhood? You came all the way from my neighborhood? You must be *crazy*. I don't think I have the strength to walk all the way back. Why didn't you just bring the food and Pepsi with you?" I protectively put Donnie's head on my shoulder.

"You think I'm *crazy*? I'm offering you and that stupid baby part of my stash and you refuse to walk back with me? You're the idiot!" The boy angrily flipped his hand in my direction and turned his back on me.

I called out to him, "I didn't mean you were crazy. I'm just too weak to walk that far, that's all. And the baby isn't stupid. He's just little." I felt tears stinging my eyes.

He turned just before he left and stared into my eyes, forcing me to look. His eyes were a cold, deep brown and the center shimmered with opalescent red. I shivered again, even more afraid.

I sat down on the pavement and rocks. I knew I shouldn't have used the word 'crazy.' I wondered why he didn't just bring the food with him. *Why did his eyes glow like that?* He was

115

horribly spiteful and mean-spirited. And how did he know our names? I would never have gone with him, especially with Donnie. I didn't trust him.

I'm glad he left, but that doesn't solve the problem of having no food or water. I can't let Donnie die.

I was close to breaking. *God, please help me! I need to find something. I need to find food or Donnie and I will both die.*

Sometimes prayers are answered, at least mine was. It was about half an hour later when I saw a big red cross on the side of a truck. *The Red Cross?* I couldn't believe it! I started to run, almost tripping over parts of buildings, wrecked automobiles, lava rocks, and mud.

I have to reach that truck. What if someone drives away before I get there? Hurry, hurry!

I made it. The truck didn't drive away. I was half crazy with relief by then, tears streaming down my face. I made it to the side of the truck and looked in the window, but there was no one inside. *Where are the other people?*

I went inside the ravaged house where the truck was parked. I yelled and I looked around for anyone to help us. There wasn't a sign of food anywhere. There wasn't a sound, only an ominous silence like in a tomb. Returning outside, I went back to the truck. I didn't see anyone.

What is going on?

I opened the truck door and climbed inside. I lay Donnie down on the front seat. Then I tore the back of the truck apart trying to find something to give the baby. *Doesn't the Red Cross carry food?*

That was when I heard the deep growl.

I turned around and the wolf was there in the front seat! This time I saw a reflection of light in his red eyes, fresh blood dripping from his mouth. I could smell the pungent odor on the wolf.

Then the knowledge of what had happened tore into me like a knife. It was Donnie's blood!

I heard myself screaming, "No! No! Leave him alone, you beast. Leave him alone!"

I knew that I was already too late. The animal ran into the woods with the blanket in his teeth.

I sat down and cried. I had failed in the one simple task for which God had spared me. He meant for me to stay alive, find Donnie, and then save him, but I had failed in taking care of Donnie just like I hadn't measured up in everything else I had done with my life. I didn't know what to do.

Do I go on like nothing happened? Like nothing mattered? Or do I lie down in the back of the truck and go to sleep?

There had to be someone ahead, but the thought still tugged at me. *Why are no people in the truck?* I told myself that maybe they had come to rescue us after the earthquake and before the volcano erupted. That had to be it. They were burned up or covered in mud like everyone else.

I walked until I thought I couldn't go on any longer. Because of the torn-up streets and the scattered debris, every foot seemed like a mile. And I was so thirsty and hungry, but I didn't pray anymore because I thought that God wasn't listening.

That was when I heard music playing. It was coming from the other side of one of the buildings. I walked over and there was a man playing a violin! It was an incredibly beautiful sound and yet, it troubled me. With every stroke of the bow on his violin, it sent haunting music throughout the countryside, evoking me to follow it.

I wondered if it were a mirage. Certainly not knowing who he was, I walked up to him slowly and reached out to touch his sleeve. He looked at me and smiled.

"What took you so long, Janie? Come inside where you can get warm. I have something for us to eat and drink."

How does he know my name? I obediently followed him.

As I stepped cautiously over the ruined opening of the door, a sudden rush of warmth caressed my face. As my foot came down, I heard it and smelled it again.

It was a guttural growl, and it carried the smell of death.

Why hadn't I expected it?

An Afterword to this story is on page 248.

13

WHEN THE DUST CLEARED

by
Sylvia Stein

All I could hear was the faint sound of a sonata playing in the background even though chaos was erupting. A crowd was running in all directions, trying to keep safe from what was happening. It was like being inside a very bad nightmare that never seemed to end.

A massive earthquake had hit our City of Angels like a bully that was running through town just ready to take anyone or anything that crossed its path. The shattering could be heard for miles and miles like a stack of dominoes falling one after another. I had to make sure that my thoughts stayed clear.

One thought came to my mind on that terrible November morning. I hoped that my fiancé John did not think that I had stood him up for our weekend trip to Napa Valley. I know it sounds silly to be worried about a date during a time like this one. I have heard in many cases when someone is going through something difficult such as this, it is good to keep happy thoughts.

As I thought about John and how he always made things better, I heard more rupturing across the Los Angeles area. I tried to keep a clear perspective, but sadly I learned that many of the homes in the suburban area of my neighborhood were destroyed, which included many of my neighbors. *Were they injured?* This was so hard to deal with because I had grown up in California. Yes, I was a valley girl.

My parents had worked hard to provide for my brother, Jacob, and me. When I got older, I moved to Los Angeles and was able to attend UCLA to pursue a career in acting. This is where I met John who was one of the directors at the Network. I still recall when I went to audition and he called my name for the first time.

"Very well done, Nadia," he smiled.

I was in complete shock.

"My name is John Gallagher. I will be directing this episode. You know, I think you were made to play this role."

After that there was no turning back. I fell madly in love.

Horrifying echoes were stirring among the street. There was damage everywhere and I could feel pain coming from every direction. I tried to stay positive by thinking about John. Another memory came to me and this time, I recalled our first anniversary of being together.

"Well, Ms. Nadia Chumsky, do you approve of this night?" he said as we danced the night away.

"Oh, I definitely approve, Mr. Gallagher," I answered with a smile.

In the midst of incredible chaos, I heard someone on a very loud intercom about to make an announcement.

"Attention, everyone, this is a message from the mayor. We are working very hard, trying to ensure your safety at this time. Most of our city has been hit pretty hard by a massive earthquake, which has also hit the surrounding cities. At this point we do not know how much of the earth still remains."

It was bad enough that I had to witness how my neighborhood was knocked down, but his words made me even sadder. I could not help but wonder how much of our world still remained.

Suddenly a horrible numbness began to overtake me, and a bad feeling began to overwhelm my thoughts. *I must think about John and focus on him!* I quickly said to myself. All I could hear in the background was a siren. Another scream came from someone who was caught up in the aftermath of this horrible event, which had affected so many. As I looked up at the sky, I saw dark clouds begin to cast a gloom and a more somber atmosphere filled the air. I tried not to panic.

I began to rush through the massive crowd. It felt like I was flying and leaping through all of them in a dream sequence that seemed to have lasted for a long time.

"Help! Help!" many of the victims cried out. I felt so helpless. I wanted to stop and carry them all out to safety, just like a soldier does in combat for his fellow man. But somehow when I tried to reach out to them, I was not able to reach them. It was like I was not in control of my own body.

Oh, John, I wish I knew if you were okay. Then out of nowhere, I began to feel the ground begin to shake again. "Oh, what is happening now? I cannot believe this!" I cried out.

Then after what seemed like forever, I began to look across the city and saw houses falling down to the ground once again. *Wait a minute! Wait a minute! I remember seeing this all before.* After a moment, I noticed I was back in my car going through traffic. "Am I losing it?" I said, trying not to freak out completely.

As I sat in my car for what seemed like hours, I still was not sure of what was happening. All of a sudden out of nowhere, I was parked outside of Andre's Restaurant where I was going to meet John. I dragged myself out of the car and saw the city skyline. One by one the buildings began to collapse around me. The only building that did not seem to be affected was the restaurant where we were supposed to meet up for our trip. Now I was more confused than ever.

"How can this be possible?" I said in a more demanding tone. "This just cannot be. Am I going mad?" In a matter of seconds, I began to hear chaos erupting once again.

As I continued to walk farther, I began to see roses on the ground. "Hmm, well this is really odd," I said in a quieter tone. But the most shocking thing that I witnessed in the middle of the path was a vineyard. This had me even more puzzled than anything. All of a sudden I was able to recognize where I was. "How can I be here?"

By this point, I was breaking inside. "Please, I need to know what is going on here!" I had been crying for a while when finally I heard a familiar voice calling to me.

"Nadia, Nadia, do not worry, babe. Everything is going to be okay now."

"John, is that you?" I asked anxiously.

"Yes," he answered.

All of a sudden I realized what had happened to our plans for a weekend trip to Napa Valley. When I was on my way to meet up with John at Andre's Restaurant, an earthquake broke out and a car had pinned me down.

"Nadia, please stay with me," he said. It was then that I started to feel really cold.

"Sir, we need to try and see if we can move her out of the car," a paramedic called out.

"No. I'm not going to leave her," John said.

"You're not helping her," a fireman said. He began the process of pulling me out of my car.

After a few moments of protesting, John finally agreed to let the first responders do their job and take me to the hospital.

I heard voices calling out to me. I was so caught up in a dream that I couldn't pay attention to anything else. I guess things started to turn around for me because all of a sudden, I felt a cool breeze enter into my body. At that moment, the only person I wanted beside me was John.

I felt grateful and relieved that both of us had survived the earthquake, even though I knew that there were many who had lost so much. I wanted to shout it out to the world.

When I woke up in my hospital room, one thing that really puzzled me was the silence. *I would think with what happened today, it would be a madhouse.* I began to get anxious because John was not with me. *I wonder what is keeping him now?*

Since it did not appear that the hospital staff was hurrying around any longer, I decided to take a stroll down the hall. But once I stepped out of the doorway, I was back in the midst of all the loud chaos.

Then the effects of an aftershock caused another building to fall. It took everything down to the ground. Once again, I was at a loss for words, feeling like I was back at square one.

"Hello? Hello!" I cried out. This seemed to be getting redundant and I was at the end of my rope. The most confusing part of all of this was that I did not understand what was happening. *Why do I keep losing John?*

As I tried to get a grip on reality, I began to hear the sound of a sonata playing in the background. It was almost like the music seemed to go into a deep crescendo, leading up to the climax of what was trying to be uncovered. I needed so desperately to know what was going on. This was not up for any negotiations. It was either now or never. I decided to take a deep breath, and plunge my way to discover the truth. With all my strength, I opened my eyes and could not believe it.

"Nadia! Nadia!" my very loving John said. He stood in my hospital room and looked into my eyes.

"Oh, John!" I said, wanting to kiss his lips. I tried to hold back my tears. "I was so frightened that I had lost you."

"Nadia, I just want you to know that I love you!" he gasped. "I always will."

I heard a loud sound that mimicked a flat line. After the sound stopped, I saw people gathering in a room. When I walked in, I noticed there were many pictures of men, women, and children. By them were names and dates.

"So, who are you here for?" an older woman asked.

"My fiancée, Nadia," John said.

I could not contain my tears any longer. *My picture is on the table? No! Not me!*

"Oh, I am so sorry," she said. "I am here for my son."

"I lost her a few days ago," John said. "The earthquake took so much from so many of us. But it took my heart away when I lost my Nadia."

It was then that I realized that I had not survived. I was dead. After all the aftermath and the chaos, I realized I had to let go of my one true love, but I didn't want to. I choked out a few words with tears flowing down my cheeks. "Goodbye, John."

It all made sense now. The journey of where I had been was all part of my denial. The answers had been clear. I just refused to see them.

"Oh, my beloved John. I will see you again. I will love you forever. I must move on to a greener pasture for now."

As I began to walk away, I started to see other souls that were headed somewhere new just like me. It was then that I began to see the humility of my life. Even though I had not quite understood what was happening, I was able to realize that once the dust had cleared, I had to learn the biggest lesson of finally letting go.

An Afterword to this story is on page 249.

14

BY THE HAND OF GOD

by
Janet Bond

The morning started like any other. Janet sat by the window drinking a cup of coffee, watching the kids head off to school. Janet liked the mornings because nothing usually happened. That's because Big B was still sleeping. Big B wasn't his real name, it stood for Big Bully. Janet wouldn't refer to him by his real name because he didn't deserve it.

As part of the neighborhood watch, Janet had lots of experience with Big B. She reported him when she saw him tagging someone's car or throwing rocks at a neighbor's window. She'd even had to step between him and the younger kids when he was threatening one of them. Those were the times that scared her. He hadn't ever hit her but she figured he would one day.

The street was empty now, just like her coffee cup, so Janet reluctantly got up to start her daily chores. By mid-morning it was getting hot, even for Chicago, so Janet closed the windows to keep in what little coolness was left in the house. She paused. Hadn't it been brighter outside a few minutes ago? A flash of lighting caused her to jump back; it was followed a few seconds later by the crash of thunder. She looked out the window; the sky was dark grey.

She flipped on the TV. There was a news reporter where there was usually a talk show. Behind the reporter was a map. It showed the whole United States and had a dozen or so red triangles on it.

"We have reports of thirteen confirmed volcanic eruptions up and down the west coast," said the reporter. "The largest of these is the Yellowstone eruption. Scientist have not developed any theories yet as to how all of these volcanoes could have started erupting this morning at the same time or why the eruptions are so strong."

Janet sat on the couch starring at the videos of the various eruptions. The reporter's words disappeared into the haze of her thoughts. "Lord, is this the end of the world? Is it doomsday? Are you destroying the world because of all the evil people?"

She pulled out of her thoughts when the reporter said, "Chicago."

"… mayor has issued a state of emergency for the greater Chicagoland area. Anyone who can leave the city and can get at least 100 miles south in the next three hours is encouraged to do so. Those who can't leave should stay in their houses with the windows closed. The pyroclastic eruption from the Yellowstone volcano should start to fall on Chicago in about three hours."

Janet ran into the bedroom and threw some clothes in a

bag. She ran to the kitchen, adding some cans of food and a can opener. She grabbed her dog, Lady, and then ran outside, jumped in her car, and backed down the driveway.

Crash. She heard something hit her car. It was Big B with a baseball bat.

"Out of the car, stool pigeon! It's time you made up for making my life so hard," he yelled at her.

The door flew open and Big B's strong arm pulled her from the car. He threw her to the ground and he jumped into the car.

"Lady!" Janet screamed.

Big B looked over at the dog siting on the seat beside him. He grabbed Lady and chucked her out the door. "Don't say I never did nothing for you." With that he stomped on the gas and sped down the street.

His mad dash didn't last long. Just around the corner were thousands of other cars trying to get down the hill. Big B swerved onto the sidewalk and made it another block before he smashed into a truck.

It took a few minutes to process what had just happened, but the scratching of Lady's paws on her leg brought Janet back. She scoped up Lady and went back into her house.

The next three hours went by slowly. She closed all the windows and put wet towels at the bottom of all the doors like they had said to do on the TV. She found her candles and filled up some containers with water. Mostly she sat watching the picture of cities that had already been destroyed and held Lady.

"Why, Lord? Why haven't you taken me home?" And

variations of it were the prayers she said under her breath. None of it seemed real.

The TV went to static a couple of minutes before rocks started to fall from the sky. Janet tried to pretend that it was hail, but soon the screams and cries from outside made that impossible. There was a knock on the door. At first Janet ignored it, but soon it was joined by other knocks.

She opened the door. Seven of her neighbors were standing there. Some were covered in blood, one person's skin had been blackened by fire, and three were kids that she watched each day on their way to school. She opened the door wide and motioned for them to come in.

While they did, Janet looked out. "Is this hell?" She asked quietly. Her neighborhood was in flames. Everywhere she looked, she could see blazing fire. Already some of the houses had collapsed in on themselves. In the distance she could see downtown, its skyscrapers lighting up the artificial night.

She shuttered.

Janet turned around and saw all the people standing in her living room. She went to them and found places for them to sit. She found her first aid kit and treated their wounds. She gave Lady to one of the little girls to hold. She told the little girl that she was to help Lady stay calm.

An hour went by and unlike the previous three hours, this one seemed to be gone in a blink. The rocks had stopped falling and the flames outside had died down. The power had gone out and now candles lit her little living room where eight people huddled together, leaving the rest of the house empty.

Janet went to the front door and peeked out. She almost

didn't believe she was looking out her front door. The ground was covered with small grey rocks, as small as a pea to as big as her fist. Thick smoke filled the air. Here and there fire could still be seen leaping from the burned out remains of a house. She kept looking for something, for some kind of hope.

"Lord, did you spare me or have you forsaken me?"

As the wind stirred up the ash and pushed the smoke around, a house became visible for a moment.

"Ms. Mary," Janet whispered. "God, let her be okay."

Janet ran to her room and found a scarf. She dipped it in water and wrapped it around her face. She went back to the front door and then stepped outside. The heat was almost unbearable and she had to fight for each breath. She slipped on some small rocks as she went down the stairs. Somehow she caught a hold of the handrail, but pain shot through her arm.

"Why do you curse me, Lord?"

She scuffled down the street towards Mary's house, stopping when she saw Big B. He was rummaging through the ashes of a neighbor's house, placing nuggets of gold and silver into his pockets, which were none other than the melted remains of rings and spoons. She watched as he pulled the ring off of a burned hand, and then she threw up.

At the noise, Big B looked over at her. "Whatcha looking at?"

"That won't do you no good where you're going," Janet said in a quiet voice.

"Mind your own business or you'll end up like old Mary,"

Big B said as he went back to his rummaging.

The color left Janet's face. She ran towards Mary's house, not worrying about falling. "Lord, let her be all right." She stumbled up her stairs and burst through the door. The room was a mess. Every drawer had been emptied onto the floor. She ran into the bedroom. There tied to the bed was Mary.

Janet sat down next to her and pulled the tape off of her mouth.

"Ms. Mary, what happened?" Janet cried as she started to untie the ropes. "Oh, God, why didn't you protect her?"

"I wouldn't tell Robert where my wedding ring is."

"Don't call him that. He's just Big B," Janet interrupted.

"And I kept telling him to leave," Mary continued. "He said I talked to much and put tape over my mouth. I tried to hit him, that's when he tied me up."

"He's still outside but I think he'll leave us alone now. He's robbing other people's houses. Come on. Let's get back to my house."

"I don't want to go. This is my house."

"You're 95 years old, Ms. Mary. You can't be living here on your own with no power or water. There are a bunch of us over at my house. We can take care of each other."

Mary gave in. She collected some of her things while Janet gathered cans from her pantry. The two of them started back up the hill to Janet's house, coughing from the smoke. The sky filled with light again as lighting bolts jumped between the clouds. Halfway up the street, the sky opened up. In all of their years the two ladies had never seen rain come down like this.

They quickly crossed the street to Janet's side as the street started to be come a river.

"Did you bring it to me?" came a voice from behind them. They looked and saw Big B coming up the sidewalk behind them. "If you give me that ring now, I just might let you live."

Mary opened her fist and looked at the small gold ring with its even smaller diamond. "My husband gave me this 75 years ago, young man. Next week would have been our anniversary. He gave it to me in love. I can't give it to you in fear."

Mary closed her fist and then threw the ring out over the waters of the street.

"Old witch!" Big B yelled as he ran to catch it before it dropped in to the water. He jumped, reached out his hand, and caught it but as he landed in the torrent, he flipped over and the ring went flying back into the air. He tried to stand but the water started to push him down the street. He crawled toward the side of the street, sliding backwards. He stopped when his back hit a car. The force of the blow knocked him down and then the water pushed him under the car.

Mary and Janet stared in horror as the water held him down.

"Oh, Lord," Janet whispered.

He frantically reached for some hand to hold but found none. The water smashed against his face and he reached a hand out toward Janet.

"Help him, Lord."

His hand dropped and disappeared under the water.

Janet turned Mary away from the car and from Big B's

body.

"Come on, Ms. Mary. We gotta get out of this rain."

They struggled against the rain and the water and then pulled themselves up the stairs to Janet's house. They looked back down the street. They watched as the car that Big B had been trapped under slid down the street and into Mary's house. The water battered against the little house and it soon crumbled. Mary collapsed to her knees.

"Ms. Mary, we gotta get inside," Janet said as she helped Mary up. They stumbled through the doorway and were greeted with an applause.

"Way to go, Mary," said one of the kids. "You killed the big bad wolf."

Janet helped Mary to the couch and went to get her a towel and some blankets. When she got back, everyone was still talking about how great it was that Big B was dead. Janet could see the sadness in Mary's eyes.

"Leave her alone," Janet said to everyone. "Big B. No, Robert, was a bully but he didn't deserve to die for it. We shouldn't be happy that he died. We should be sad that he died and that so many other people died too. If you want to be happy 'bout something, be thankful we're still alive."

One of the little girls, Jill, started to cry. Janet went to her and picked her up.

"I want my mommy," she sobbed into Janet's shoulder.

"I know. It's okay to cry. Cryin's good for the soul," said Janet in a hushed voice.

"Give her here," Mary said, "you've got other things to take care of. Let me do something I'm good at. Besides, I need to do a little cryin' myself.

Janet set Jill onto Mary's lap and the two of them clung to each other for many hours. Janet busied herself getting food for everyone and finding enough blankets. The rain kept falling all night and into the next day. When sunlight finally came through the drapes, it was late afternoon. The world outside had changed again. The floodwaters had washed away many of the rocks and most of the ash. All but Janet's house lay in ruins.

The world inside of Janet's house had changed even more. Instead of being part of a neighborhood watch that just reported on the bullies, they were a neighborhood that had cared for each other. They had shared their food, their grief, their fears, and their hopes as well.

Through the silence outside, void of cars and people and airplanes flying overhead, the sound of a helicopter cut cleanly. Every heart jumped and then they ran outside, except for Janet who stayed to help Mary stand up. From the porch the two of them watched this new family wave down the helicopter, wondering what life would be like now and feeling thankful that they wouldn't have to face it alone.

"Thank you, Lord, for never leaving us," Janet prayed as she watched the helicopter land.

An Afterword to this story is on page 250.

15

LIVING IN THE SHADOW

by
Douglas G. Clarke

"Repent! Repent! The end is here!"

The preacher's voice reached me through the rubble that once has been the town of Siletz, Oregon. I shivered at the words. Not because of the words, but because over the last five weeks he had been right.

I looked for any new smoke plumes. Due east, Mount Hood continued to smolder; it had been the first to go, taking Portland with it. To the southeast, the Three Sisters belched ash into the air. They had sent pumice the size of VW bugs raining down on my neighborhood. Farther to the south there was evidence of Newberry, McLoughlin, Medicine, and Lassen's activity. Six volcanoes erupted, each after the preacher had walked through town announcing that the end was here.

Looking back toward the east I studied the barely visible peak of Mount Jefferson and relaxed a bit. No activity there.

But even so, I was wary. Jefferson was the closest one that could erupt and send lava steams down the Siletz River to wipe us out.

As the preacher's voice faded away, I returned to my work, the impending doom suppressed by the needs at hand. I moved away the last of the debris and found my prize, boxes of food. Most of the food had been destroyed by the fire, but the cans still might be good. I stacked the blackened treasure in my pack, wondering what surprise each might hold.

I struggled during the walk back to my house. The weight on my back was more than I should have carried but less than what my family needed to survive. A cloud of ash followed me, and I stumbled whenever my foot struck something hidden beneath the grey blanket.

I reached home as the sun was setting. I use to think my neighbors' houses were too close to mine, but not after my house was the only house left on C Street. In fact, after the last erupted, I had the only house left in Siletz.

My son waved to me from the second story window. I returned the wave and then stumbled, almost falling. I saw Jake laughing. Anger flared up in me, but then I saw Jake fall off the chair he must have been standing on. Quickly he popped back out the window and was laughing even harder. I couldn't help but smile. I thanked God that my son could laugh after all we'd gone through.

He disappeared from the window, and I could hear his muffled voice calling down to his mom. The door opened and I saw my beautiful, if disheveled wife, Beth, waiting for me. She helped me get my pack off and then wrapped her arms around me. It sure was nice coming home.

"We have company," Beth said.

I smiled and nodded my head. We had agreed the day after the town had been destroyed and our house had been spared, that God must have a reason. The next day when someone knocked on our door and asked to spend the night, we figured that was the reason. God had given us the gift of hospitality and the means to share that gift with others. Since that second day, there had been a steady stream of refuges heading south.

Not every night, but most nights, someone knocked on our door. Some traveled by car, others on foot. Some had food with them, but some hadn't eaten for days. Most came through Lincoln City, deciding to travel inland instead of trying to get down the coast. We had one family a couple weeks ago that had come all the way from Salem.

As I cleaned up, the aroma from Beth's cooking enticed me. It made me hurry to join them. Everyone sat around the table talking, so I quietly joined them.

"Here's my husband, Henry. These are the Walkers, Jim and Sue, and their daughter, Mary," Beth said.

I nodded to each one of them. "Glad to meet you. Have you been on the road long?"

"We were just talking about that," Beth said. "They're from Portland and have been traveling since the day Mount Hood and Mount Adams erupted."

"That's right," Jim said. "I can't even begin to describe what it was like. Every road was packed with cars, all stopped with nowhere to go. I pulled our car to the side of the road and we started walking. We decided to head for higher ground and walked up into the woods to the west of town."

"When Hood exploded, we could feel the rumbling. It kept growing louder and louder for several hours. Then we saw a wall of water and ash coming down Columbia River. It must have been a hundred feet tall. We watched, not knowing what to do as the city disappeared. All those people sitting in their cars." Jim shuttered.

"Where are you headed?" Beth asked, jumping in.

Sue mouthed *thank you* when Jim sat with his eyes closed. "We have family in Jenner. That's near San Francisco. We got word from them four weeks ago, and they were still fine."

"That's a long way," said Jake.

"A little over 550 miles. Longer if we have to make detours."

The conversation continued as we ate. The Walkers told us about getting out of Portland, their journey to the sea, and how some people along the way were helpful while others were cruel. Their descriptions finally came to their impressions of Siletz.

Sue said, "We had been traveling all day through the burned-out forest. Then we came over a small rise and saw a band of green. When we got closer we came to a bridge over a river just outside of town. On the other side was a row of trees hugging the riverbank. It was so wonderful to see green after so many days of grey and black."

"We crossed over the bridge and that's when we saw a man, all dressed in black," Jim said.

"The preacher," Beth said, emphasizing the title.

"He was telling us to repent and that the end had come."

"That's what he does," Jake shood his head slightly and met Beth's eyes.

"Then he said we had to give him three cans of food, one for each of us so we could travel through purgatory. We showed him that we only had two cans left, but he made us give him both."

Beth, Jake, and I just nodded.

The conversation turned to hopes and dreams of what our lives could be again. Jake ran and brought back his guitar. He played some songs. It was nice to be with new people and share our lives. Jake and I cleaned the table and I showed our guests to their room for the night.

I was the last one awake, standing by my bedroom window looking east. I didn't want to believe that another disaster was coming, but I had heard the preacher calling out during the day. I scanned the horizon seeing only the blackness, remembering how the lights of Salem use to pollute the sky. I missed those lights.

A little past four in the morning the rumbles started. I jumped from bed and ran to the window. Mount Jefferson. The sky was bright to the east. It lit up from the glow of lava as it ran down the mountainside and burning rocks were thrown into the air.

I woke Beth and then the others, hurrying them downstairs as the first cinders bounced off the roof. I could tell young Mary was scared, hanging from her father's neck. I was scared too.

"Don't worry, Mary," I said in my most comforting and assuring voice. "We've been through this several times." From the look on her face, I don't think she believed me.

Once we reached the cellar and I turned on a lantern, Jim pulled me aside. "Shouldn't we get to higher ground?"

"Maybe. But the pumice raining down right now is the size of baseballs and soccer balls. We wouldn't last a minute out there, and we don't have anywhere to go."

"But…what happened in Portland…we're in a valley here. They were all covered."

I put a hand on his shoulder and squeezed it gently. "We've been through this lots of times, and each time our house has been spared. That's why we're still here. God has to be sparing our house for a reason, and we believe it is because we can help travelers like you."

We waited out the eruption. By noon the rocks stopped falling from the sky. We ventured upstairs to see how our world had changed. Outside the ground was covered with another foot of rocks and ash. Most of the rocks were small, but a few were as big as cars. Inside we found a couple of new holes in the roof, but nothing I couldn't fix.

We went out on the balcony and looked towards Jefferson. Only a thin trail of smoke marked the violence of last night, that and the new cone, standing to the right of Jefferson.

"What do you think they'll call it?" Jake asked when it disappeared in a flash of fire and ash

"Cellar!" I yelled, and we all ran. I don't know why I was so panicked. We had several minutes, but I ran anyway. Almost seven minutes later when we heard the first of the pea-sized rocks hitting the house, but this time they weren't falling from the sky. They were lava bullets fired from the largest volcano gun on earth.

As we huddled in the cellar, the windows shattered upstairs. A minute later the sound wave reached us. The explosion was deafening. Jake was lying on the ground, with his hands pressed against his ears, crying to himself. Moments later the shock wave reached us, adding the sound of our house being perforated.

It felt like forever, but the explosion ended and our house was still standing. To say that the house had seen better days would have been an understatement of earth shattering proportions. Considering the world had just been shattered, no one wanted to risk saying anything.

Every window was gone—not just broken, but gone. There were holes in the walls where rocks had traveled all the way through the house. Every glass and plate had been shattered. But somehow our house remained standing.

We spent the next hour cleaning up, putting plastic on the windows, picking up rocks, and sweeping up ash. The Walkers joined in and helped us. Then Beth called us down for lunch—green beans, peaches, and sloppy joe sauce with no meat.

In the afternoon I went up on the roof and patched the holes, glad I had planned on replacing so I had boxes of shingles on hand. The Walkers decided to stay a couple of extra days and help us put things back together. Jim figured three days wouldn't make any difference adding to the length of their trip.

Rain came down hard the day they left. It was a dirty rain

full of ash, but it was still cleaner than Siletz. We gave them a few cans of food to eat as they traveled, and three extra in case they ran into the preacher again. Though we hadn't seen him since Jefferson blew.

I walked them to the bridge leading out of town. The river was thick with ash. I explained how to get to Toledo and then to Newport. I wished them luck and then waited for them to reach the bend. Mary waved to me, and I waved back until they disappeared.

I resumed searching for cans of food in my methodical way. All the time wondering why I wasn't headed down that road with them. It wasn't too late. I could run back and get Beth and Jake. But I didn't. I just collected more cans and some new glasses.

On the way back home, I saw a deer nibbling on some grass shoots that were pushing up through the ash. Jake was waiting for me, waving to me from the second story window. I waved back.

That's when I realized...I was where I was supposed to be...home.

An Afterword to this story is on page 251.

16

THE UNWELCOME GUEST

by
Gail Harkins

From space, the Pacific Rim appeared as a jeweled necklace. After the first eruption in New Zealand, the volcanic glow spread northward through Indonesia to Japan and, most recently, the Kamchatka Peninsula. In the Americas, eruptions began at Chile's southern tip, progressing through the Andes into Mexico and up the Sierra Nevadas.

When California's Long Valley Caldera exploded, my university in Washington went on hiatus and Dad sent me to live on the peninsula with Uncle Todd and Aunt Ellen, where I would be safe. In their ranch house, watching the spectacle on TV, we were transfixed by the terrible beauty that would soon destroy our world. When the earth trembled and our screen went black, we knew it was our turn to endure.

The first blast shot ash 20 kilometers into the sky as lava swept over towns near Mount Rainier, and the surrounding forests blazed, then smoldered. Telecommunications were severed. We could only watch the skies and wait. Later when the lava flows approached our area, they followed their ancient paths to the sea, scorching the *asbestos forest* and obliterating the single highway that linked the peninsula to the mainland. The once-mighty river that coursed westward atop ancient flows vaporized, buried by this new, steaming onslaught.

Eventually there was little left to burn. In time, the lichen and fireweed took hold in the depleted forests. Deer and elk ventured down from the mountains, followed by the cougars that fed on them and finally, the people.

* * *

"Hello!" A grungy figure called out as he emerged from the still-forested ridgeline that was now the entrance to our property. Uncle Todd, surrounded by dogs, shouldered his shotgun and strode to the edge of the clearing.

"Got some water?" the stranger asked.

"Lake's that way, a quarter mile." He pointed east.

"Lake!?"

"Lava dammed the river. The whole valley's underwater now."

"Then my house is gone." The stranger paused. "I'm Lem Bastardi. I lived along the river."

Uncle Todd took in his torn pack with the frayed sunburst embroidered on the flap, his matted beard and greasy hair. "I thought you were back East."

Lem ignored him and turned to the porch where I stood in jeans and a T-shirt. "Gonna invite me in? I had a long hike getting here. Your wife," he nodded to me, "might want some news from the outside world."

"She's not my wife."

"Well, then." He smiled for the first time. It didn't extend to his eyes.

Uncle Todd let Lem sit on the porch and signaled me to bring a cool drink. Instead, gray-haired Aunt Ellen carried out a pitcher and two glasses. Butterscotch, my calico cat, stayed on the porch and entwined himself around Uncle's legs before hopping into his lap.

"Ellen, take this bundle of fluff inside, will you?"

She picked up the cat and returned to the kitchen where I waited.

"Do you know him?" I asked.

She nodded grimly. "He's trouble, by the name of Lemuel Bastardi!"

My brows furrowed.

"A former neighbor," she explained. "He went to prison for sexual assault. I hoped they'd keep him."

"Rape?"

Aunt Ellen nodded grimly. "Statutory rape. A young girl from town. A family friend, I heard. Sad business. I didn't think he'd have the gall to come back here."

"Then why's Uncle Todd even talking to him?"

She shook her head. "Heaven only knows."

* * *

Lem made his camp a mile down the bluff on the shore above his former home. My uncle took me there the next day when we were foraging for chanterelles, so I'd know exactly where it was. He sat with his back to us, suspending a fishing pole over the lake.

"Catching anything?" Uncle Todd asked.

Lem turned and eyed me from head to toe, letting his gaze linger a bit too long before flicking his eyes to my uncle. "Got a steelhead on a stringer. If I get a couple more, I'll cut some alder and smoke' em. Maybe bring you some."

"That'd be nice. My niece and I brought you some mushrooms and salal berries. The berries don't taste like much, but we lived on them after the blast. They'll go well with the fish."

"And the mushrooms?" His eyebrows rose quizzically.

"She's a botanist. They're safe."

As we left, I felt his eyes on me, sizing me up, as we retraced our steps through charred woods that were beginning to green with saplings and fiddleback ferns.

When we were well out of earshot, I finally asked what I had been dying to know. "Aunt Ellen told me he was a rapist. Why do you even talk to him, much less bring him food?"

He was quiet so long I thought he'd forgotten my question. Finally, he answered. "I want to know the man's intentions. Keep your friends close and your enemies closer, eh?" He winked at me.

Later that morning as I rinsed volcanic dust from the fruits of our foraging, Uncle Todd came into the kitchen and sat at the table. "Laurel, stop what you're doing a moment and come here."

He placed a pistol on the table.

"If Lem's back, others will follow. From now on, you keep this with you at all times. Put it in a pocket. You step outside, you have it with you. You're here in the house—especially if you're alone—you have it on you." He looked at my aunt. "You too, Ellen. That man's bad news."

He turned his attention back to me. "Laurel, do you remember how to use it?"

"I remember, but is it really necessary?"

"Better safe than sorry."

* * *

I was deep in the salal bushes that covered the slope above the house the next day when I heard him, soft-footing along an old deer trail.

"Here, kitty, kitty. Come to old Lem," he coaxed. I saw a flash of fur as Butterscotch scooted underneath a log and disappeared. I fingered the pistol in my pocket and crouched in the bushes, waiting for him to leave. I sat there a long time.

Lem appeared on our driveway the next day, about an hour before dinner time. "I brought you some fish," he called from a distance. The shimmering steelhead trout he held looked like it would measure nearly 30 inches from tip to tail.

"Thank you," Uncle Todd replied. "It'll make a nice addition to the stew. You'll join us for dinner, of course."

147

"Why, thank you. I don't mind if I do." Lem's words were polite but his eyes flitted around the house, taking in every detail.

We sat on the stone patio above our pond, enjoying the faint breeze that made the clouds scuttle overhead and revealed occasional glimpses of blue. Aunt Ellen and I ferried bowls of steelhead stew from the kitchen and a pitcher of salmonberry cider we had made last spring.

Finally, he leaned back and grinned. "This is a fine dinner, Ellen, Laurel. I appreciate it. Much better than my bachelor dinners."

My aunt and I just looked at each other and waited for him to continue.

He turned to Uncle Todd. "How'd you all get along after the blast?"

As my uncle recounted the fires that burned much of the forests and the floods that sent low-lying communities fleeing into the hills, Butterscotch hopped into my lap and nibbled a morsel of fish from my fingers.

"Dark days. You must have had plenty to eat, though. You kept that cat." His eyes darted lecherously to my lap, where Butterscotch purred contentedly. "Looks like he's in a fine position." His gaze shifted upward, but never reached my face.

I clutched my cat protectively. "Butterscotch is mine." My voice had a hard edge that seemed to surprise Lem. "No one hurts him. No one. Is that understood?" I had loved Butterscotch since he was kitten, some 14 years ago.

"My apologies, if I've offended. It's just that I saw him up in the hills the other day, away from the house," he backpedaled. "You might want to keep a closer eye on him, if you don't want him to get hurt."

"Is that a threat?" I asked.

He leered at me. "Just some friendly advice. That's all. Just some friendly advice."

I turned to my aunt and uncle. "Excuse me." I pushed back my chair and retreated to the house with Butterscotch in my arms.

"Somebody needs to take that girl down a notch," Lem commented under his breath.

Uncle Todd and Aunt Ellen stood together. "Lem, it's time for you to go."

* * *

Lem kept his distance for the next few weeks and I kept Butterscotch inside, at least inside as much as possible. A natural hunter, he hated being cooped up and cried pitifully. Finally, I relented and let him out one night. I was rewarded in the morning with a pile of mice and voles by my bedroom door. Meat was still scarce despite the occasional deer. Aunt Ellen and I added hawksbeard roots, chanterelles, and some greens to Butterscotch's offering for a stir-fry. After about a week of Butterscotch's gifts, I awakened to find his spot on my bed empty. I watched for him throughout the day, but he didn't return.

The following morning, I slipped my pistol into my pocket and went searching for him. If he was in the salal bushes, he didn't answer. The old orchard, where he liked to sun himself during our increasingly clear days, was empty. The hollowed-out cedar stump, where he liked to cat-nap, was vacant.

Desperation and the sight of smoke lured me to Lem's camp. I approached silently, cautiously circling round to the south rather than taking the direct path from the north. He'd been trapping. Something, a rabbit perhaps, roasted on a spit above his campfire. He sat near the lake, scrapping a hide. I moved closer, until I saw the beautiful calico fur. I gasped, but he continued scraping.

"It's just a cat. A mangy, flea-ridden cat," he said, still with his back to me.

"He's my cat! And he doesn't have fleas!"

The pistol was in my hand. He was in my sights.

* * *

Aunt Ellen's arms were wrapped around me, trying to stop my shaking, when Uncle Todd came through the door. He sized up the situation in a glance.

"It was Lem." Aunt Ellen told him what had happened as I gulped for air between sobs.

"I couldn't pull the trigger, Uncle Todd. I wanted to, but I couldn't do it."

Aunt Ellen gave me a glass of water.

Uncle Todd put his hand on my shoulder, in an attempt at comfort. "It's probably for the best, child. It's a terrible thing to live with—killing a man."

I looked into blue eyes riddled with sadness and saw empathy. "It's not done lightly," I agreed.

He took a long drink of the salmonberry cider my aunt poured, then wiped his mouth with the back of his hand. "Tomorrow morning, I'm going to have a visit with that man. It's time for him to git."

I gazed up at him with gratitude.

That night, I lay in my bed and thought about Butterscotch, Uncle Todd, and Lem Bastardi. My tears turned to anger. "That no-good, dirty, rotten piece of filth! He's gotten away with it. When he leaves here, he'll just cause trouble somewhere else—and probably more than just killing somebody's pet. Sorry, Butterscotch." I touched the empty pillow near my head where he had slept.

Before dawn, I was up and out of the house. When I returned, my basket was filled with psilocybe mushrooms. Their thin slivers bled blue as I sliced them. Carefully, I stirred the mushrooms into a pan along with wild garlic and onions, and leaves from hawksbeard, a type of dandelion. It was a typical stew for this area, at least after the eruption.

"Ummm. Something smells good." Uncle Todd stepped into the kitchen and reached for a spoon.

"No!" I batted it out of his hand. "I made this specially for Lem. I picked the mushrooms this morning. You understand? Just for Bastardi. Maybe he'll leave faster if he's not travelling on an empty stomach."

Uncle Todd eyed me speculatively. "Maybe you're right. A present to speed him on his way. Specially for Lem."

"And only Lem," I stressed.

Fog was rising as Uncle Todd strapped on his .45. I poured the stew into a bladder, knotted the top, and handed it to him.

Lem was sharpening his knife when Uncle Todd stepped into the clearing around the campsite.

"Lemuel Bastardi, we've got to talk."

"I'm listening." Smoke from the campfire blew between them.

"You've been eyeing my niece. I don't like it. Yesterday you killed her cat. I don't like that, either. It's past time for you to git."

Lem leaned back and tested the blade, then looked lazily at Uncle Todd. "Heck, her little pet got caught in one of my snares. She should've taken better care. Seemed a shame to waste it and I was hungry."

Uncle Todd eased his jacket back, showing the pistol. "Game's more plentiful up in high country. Head north. Fill your belly there. This should tide you over." Uncle Todd handed him the bladder of mushroom stew.

"I'll give you an hour to pack up and be on your way. I'll be checking." He patted his pistol and disappeared into the early morning fog.

Uncle Todd sat behind a copse of charred trees as Lem grumbled and packed. He headed north as instructed, following the new shoreline. When the fog lifted and the sun was high, he stopped for lunch where a stream trickled into the lake. As he stood to continue his journey, he tottered. Gradually, his steps became less sure. He began throwing his knifes at non-existent deer formed from the burnt-out stumps of the once grand forest. When the convulsions started, he began raving, convinced he was about to die. Trembling, he approached the lake, put his face to the water and drank deeply.

* * *

Summer turned to fall. The deer returned to the ridge, as Uncle Todd had predicted, nibbling the new grass that stayed green into winter in the mild climate. We gave thanks, then smoked their meat. This winter, we would eat well. When the geese flew through the night, Aunt Ellen visited a friend across the ridge and returned with a brown and tan striped kitten. I named her Taffy, my second-favorite candy. She slept on my pillow, like Butterscotch.

The mountain peaks were blanketed with snow, and the first flakes were fluttering through our own lowland skies when two hunters stepped out of the tree-line and made for our house.

"John, Sam, it's good to see you. What's the news?" Aunt Ellen welcomed them into a kitchen warm with the aroma of roasting grouse.

"The hunting's good up toward the old dam," John began.

"Be careful though. The big cats are getting active," Sam added. "We found a body dragged into some deep brush a couple miles south of the old bridge. Flesh was pretty much gone."

My uncle and I looked at each other. "Any idea who it was?"

Sam shrugged. "All we found was a scrap of canvas with a sunburst on it. It could've been anybody."

An Afterword to this story is on page 252.

THE WILD REMAINS

by
Amos Parker

Heat.

It is not a word in his mind.

Unbearable heat.

It is a feeling. It is a sensation. It is a straining, wolfish certainty.

I am dressed wrong for it.

These are almost wordless times.

It may be a thought, if not a word. It may be thinking, if the red, liquid rocks from the bowels of the Earth left any thoughts alive in the hissing land, and if he can be said to be a creature capable of thoughts at all. He may be such a creature now. He may have been such a creature in the past. Or the complicated soft ones the world has butted him against may own thought, as they believe they own the world they burned in their own way before it chose to burn itself, as if to spite them.

I hunger.

Nothing but words can tell us the story of cataclysm, or any story at all.

Standing in the toothless mouth of the cave, he looks down the charred hill. The smoke is dying out of the heat of the air. He could breathe, for the immeasurable time, only in the deep, cool cave where the trickling water has now run out. He can now breathe outside, as the red liquid rocks seem to fall asleep, altering to a hard, solid grey. Almost everywhere a new ground is forming, close to lifeless and almost without green, and with little for hunger to spur a run towards.

And I thirst.

There may be nothing to spur a run against that. Much of the death-scented smoke is, in truth, the up spirited steam of water. It runs from him, as if to the steam that billows high in the blue.

Why? And what.

His stead yellow gaze surveys the landscape. His eyes bloom with irises like molten gold. They blink without fear, without future, and without thought. The now is the key. He turns, too thin under his grey coat, and surveys the dark, now cooler interior of the cave as if his family may still be there, watching him with molten gold of their own from out of the silver past. But his mate and his offspring do not look back out at him, from the black cave mouth that is like death and contains nothing anymore in its bowels to sate hunger or thirst.

That death black mouth, or another, ate them. And so he turns away once more, offering it only what may be a thought.

Not today.

And now he surveys, through the steam, smoke and ended life.

To the right, and miles away though he does not measure, grows the impossible and blessed remains of a stand of high green trees he can see through the smoke. It is on a hill, as is his cave, and so has somehow been spared by the flows of red liquid rock that sought the low places that water seeks also. Or sought, before it ran.

And then there is the other.

He swings his long face away. To the left, and as many miles away though he still does not measure, squats a jarring and unnatural trio of the fragile once-tree caves built by the complicated soft ones who hoard value. They too crouch on the crown of a third hill, saved from the fate of the other wooden dens that vanished in screaming fire.

Choose.

He swings his long, family-stripped face from right to left and back again. The now and its present path to the future sing to him. There may be no more complicated danger anymore, to the left. It is a wordless and uncomplicated fading of worry.

High in the fading smoke of the sky, there is the blue, as before, though the smoke runs to it as the water does. The high-travelling and feminine globe of molten gold sinks, almost at the mouth of its secret cave beneath all things. The Golden Mother is settling into the surviving forest. But she will not burn them, will not bring the fire that the booming yellow forks can bring, or that the departing, once-boiling stone brought. She never burns them, but only boons them.

157

She follows no lead, but only leads that what she sees may follow. She is a breed of replacement for his mate and children, but has nothing to learn from, or offer to, the land beneath her hot, invisible paws.

She abides. She does no more.

Curiosity. It burns hot and victorious.

He will do what is left and not what is right: the once-trees before the still. He will seek for freed hoards.

Lifting his grey-clothed head, his long ears lay against his lifting head. The grey fur that is his clothing has molted some. Swinging his head away from the right and off to the left, he howls that way, for the Silver Father always emerges as the Golden Mother hides. His still-white teeth come near to glowing, and then with the true and easy lupus lope as grey as the stone, he travels down to what is left of the remains.

Begin.

* * *

The hiss and smoke of the ground has come near to spending itself, like a season's leaves, and the strong scent of deep things from the Golden Mother's secret, burning cave beneath fades on a new sweet breeze from somewhere special.

It is almost too hot for pads and claws.

He goes down into valleys. Sometimes there is a path. Sometimes it is cool. When those sometimes are missed, his paws burn.

Such thirst. Such.

He pants, long pink tongue lolling as he sniffs the breeze,

low and stalking. The valleys infect the new, sweet breeze with the old sulfurous odors. Air blows from the direction of his den but does not carry the scent of kin. His burdensome fur bristles as an instinct tells him that the complicated, two-legged soft ones will smell him coming, if any still live. But then he remembers that they have that near blindness of smell and do not scent things coming unless they come hard and close. With an effort he calms himself, and his fur flattens once more.

His feet are too hot. They burn, but he must endure, for thirst burns too. Under his feet, there rock as grey as him is smooth. There is little sharpness to cut him.

The once-tree dens, in the dangerous open of the air, are still alien things of complexity and full of ominous purpose. Shapes with straight lines decorate them, and pieces appear to be missing, exposing interiors. They loom with unnatural color.

The miles melt unmeasured, as the rocks did. They will harden again, as miles do, when new destinations call.

Cave carcasses.

Many charred black remains of other dens smolder nearby in the lowlands. Some dark bones stick from out of the new stone. All of it is still distant, and he stalks beyond the reach of any living eyes possessed by two-legged soft ones.

Death is not complicated.

But he sees them. They are not all dead. He stops.

In the jumble of their dens he sees them walking, weak for many reasons and carrying their awful exploding sticks that both build and tear down fear. He hears their strange calls, their jumbling voices that are just one owned complexity.

His feet hurt. Worse. On a cool patch he lies down, licking them.

Water.

Before he rises up again, the breeze changes. The current from his den is defeated by a stronger one from theirs and it brings him their dirty, clumsy scents but also carries uncomplicated creatures into his nose that he knows. Animals. His four-legged soft cousins are among them in the air.

And water.

Water! Life!

His dry, starved form trembles. His bowels quiver. His thick blood screams.

The grey one prowls around the hill, in a circle and at a distance and looking at the cluster of promises on the hilltop. The new, foul breeze seems to move with him, always carrying the stench and sweetness. His feet burn again, and so in a cool patch he lies still to lick them again. Where is the stream? His thoughts flow like the imprisoned water he smells, waterfalls in his mind, and he catches breaths of their weak urine.

Birds. Cattle. Rats.

Food. It follows water.

Pricking up his ears, he listens as the wind aids him. He hears a bark. It continues, and it does not stop.

"Shut up your stupid mutt! Shut him up, Max, or I'll shut him up for you and turn him into jerky. We've lost enough, and I'm not going to lose my hearing!" Mr. Smith yells.

"Don't you touch my dog, Mr. Smith!" Max cries out.

"Max, son," Mother says. "Let your daddy settle this.

Stay out of it."

"Touch my son's dog and I'll turn *you* into jerky!" Ted says. "Lost? You wanna talk about lost? You're the one threatening my son that he's going to lose his dog!"

"Jane, come here!" Mother shouts.

The dog's barking continues.

"I mean it! Shut up your mutt!" Mr. Smith threatens.

"Put your gun down. We've got three small kids out here!" Ted points.

"Pa!" the youngest boy, Melvin Smith, Mr. Smith's only son, calls out. "Our house!"

"You stay out of this, Melvin! This is a man's business!" Mr. Smith says.

"Our house! It's gone, Pa!" Melvin cries out.

"Melvin! Stay back!" Max's mother, Molly, instructs.

Max's dog growls.

Mr. Smith gives another threat. "Call off your dog or I'll shoot him!"

"Now, don't be stupid," Ted says.

"Daddy!" Jane calls out.

"No, Jane! Stay back!"

Max's dog continues to growl.

The grey one bristles. It is his cousin against the soft ones, and the barking calls to him. Without a family, what does he have but cousins?

I need to help. But… danger!

"Get away, you dumb mutt! Ow! Go away!" Mr. Smith yells out, kicking at Max's dog to stay back.

"Pa!" Max cries out as his dog begins to whine. "Don't

kick my dog, Mr. Smith!"

"Your dumb dog bit me!" Mr. Smith fumes.

"Put your shotgun down! We can work this out like men!"

"No! Enough of this! If you won't take care of it, I will!" Mr. Smith says.

Boom!

"You idoit! You stupid dog-killing monster!" Max yells.

"Daaaaaaaaddy!" Jane screams.

"Jane, calm down!" Ted says.

"Now you've got some food, Max," Mr. Smith jokes. "Your dog was good for something."

The grey one bristles again, with the smell of a cousin's blood. He could have protected his cousin. Or no. Not against the exploding sticks. He would be in a pool of blood now too. Would he be with his family?

For a long time, he listens to the noise of the complicated, two-legged soft ones fighting. Within the noise and the chaos, birds squawk and cattle moan, and he even discerns the sound of rats squeaking and clawing in rock dens under the wooden dens, where they nibble grain.

And water, the scent ever exploding in his nose. Always the smell of water, somehow, somewhere, bursting and crashing with waves in his mind. It overpowers every other smell, even the blood of his cousin, and the thickness of his own blood howls skyward for it. The aroma of water flows like the great river and its destination lake, leaping with glistening fish that tease, spin, and vanish again. Food after.

But it is only the scent. He must approach.

The very different and unreachable promise of it flares in his pumping, viscous blood. It is a mystery. The absence of water burns like the presence of fire.

Such fury!

His ears prick up as the sky darkens and the fighting ends. He knows all of the two-legged soft ones will vanish into their once-tree dens to sleep. The Silver Father does not maintain day. The grey one knows the two-legged ones sleep the sleep of the dead, and he marvels at the resultant survival.

And, in time, they do vanish into their dens. The faint traces of stars appear through the overhead smoke, with the fat face of the Silver Father shedding silver light, and when the husbanded animals fall silent too, he stalks again. His senses sharpen.

Silence.

The deadening smoke clears still further, blowing off on a firmer breeze toward the trees growing on the hill behind which the Golden Mother departed.

All he hears is the faint hiss of the still-cooling stone ground.

And rats. Chewing.

Careful.

Unimpeded, he lopes into the vast open space contained by the three once-tree dens. Pens hold a small animal den, out of which comes the scent of fowl. Opposite him is a fence surrounding cattle. Close by is a pool of cooling, drying, sinking blood.

In the dead center of the dirty expanse, stared down upon by dark holes in the walls of the great dens, is a circle of rising stones bound together, covered with a roof of once-trees. A thin cord of something and a bar join, the cord joined to a small thing shaped like the stones. The thing rests on the rim of the bound stones.

It is from up out of the stones that the scent of sweet water comes, as if on the sweetest of springtime breezes. The body of his cousin, his brother, is gone.

Meat will wait.

He forgets the blood of the dog.

Drink!

Loping, he comes nearer to the high ring of stones and is drowned in sensation.

Silver Father and Golden Mother the water smell!

A kind of insanity begins, up out of his blood as a blue, crystalline geyser might, and flowing with it into his mind. Feelings, fueling a breed of desperation unlike any he has ever known, drowns him. Some ancient ancestral instinct gives him new kinship with the fish that swim.

In his drowning is his mate and his pups. They are burned black and dry. The wetness is too late for them to drink, or even swim in. They sink.

Heedless with the blindness of the insanity, he hurtles across the dust to the stone. Burned pads, already cracked, let dust into themselves. At the source, still more insane, he vaults his front paws onto the lip and, stretching over, he looks down.

Where?

The smell is the dry blood of insanity itself. He sees darkness, like the cave mouth that swallowed his family and that wants to swallow him.

Where is it?

And, leaning further in, his shoulder strikes the bucket and, with a horrible clattering wooden clacking it tumbles down into the well. Splash!

* * *

"What was that noise?"

Animal sounds are heard outside of the homes of the people. Chickens wake, clucking and flapping. Woken cows moo, catching the scent of their own fear. Beams of sullied golden light lance out of the windows. Struck by them, the grey one jolts back and feels the dust on all burning paws.

"Wolf! Molly! There's a wolf!" Ted calls out to his wife.

"What? Where?"

"There's a wolf in the courtyard!"

"It'll kill the chickens!"

Max is concerned. "Dad! What about the cows?"

"Yes, the cows too! Get the gun!" Ted instructs.

"I put it away! After Jed shot my dog!"

"What?" Ted is disturbed by this news.

"Mommy!" Jane feels afraid.

"Keep away from it!" Molly tells the three kids.

"Quiet, everyone! Go get the gun, Max, before the wolf gets our chickens and our cows!"

The wolf is unwilling to leave the scent of blessed water.

No! Die! No! Dive!

"There it is! I'll shoot it before it runs off or it'll stalk us forever!" Mr. Smith says.

It presses itself to the bonded circle of stones, bristling and growling as though protecting a fallen deer from a rival pack of wolves now dead. The smell tethers it.

Mine!

The wolf is blinded. The enemy is lances of impure golden rays of light. A door crashes open, banging, and Jed stumbles out into the courtyard. His rifle rests across his chest on the diagonal, like the handle of some handhold without a shield. Max emerges too, his shotgun cocked.

"I've got him," Mr. Smith says with a clear aim.

The wolf imagines the captive dog it smelled before.

"Shoot next to it to scare it away!" Ted says.

"No, don't kill it, Daddy. It's just thirsty. Let it drink!" Jane is standing near.

Ted calls out to Mr. Smith. "You already killed one canine! Let's scare this one off."

"This one is mine." Mr. Smith lifts the rifle, aiming at the wolf. "You little monster. You hunting for food? Or are you hunting for us? Either way, you're dead today."

The blinded wolf does not understand. Yet something, some instinct overriding its blue, liquid insanity, makes it bolt in time.

Boom! The rifle cracks like thunder, shattering stone. But the wolf is gone. Boom! The shotgun cracks. The wolf feels something part the grey fur of its tail. But the pain has not pierced his skin. The pain is in his hot feet as the sound rushes through his blood, making him run fast.

Run... like water!

The sound of wood splintering from bullets impact echoes in the confines. Another shot, but the wolf is gone.

"Let's chase it, Ted! I'll bring the flashlight!" Mr. Smith says.

"Molly?" Ted calls out to his wife, then turns to Mr. Smith. "We can't chase it. Not out there. Not at night."

Molly calls out to her husband. "Let it go, Love!"

"We can't let it get away!" Mr. Smith says.

"Oh, yes, we can!" Ted says.

"We have to chase it! Track it down!" Mr. Smith says.

"Daddy!" Jane calls out. "Don't leave us!"

Long gone, the wolf can still hear the chaos.

Ted lets the wolf go. "It'll die out there, someday. He's searching for water. Let's get back to sleep."

* * *

A long journey by the light of the Silver father brings him, panting, to the remains of the trees. Crickets chirp. An owl hoots. The ground is mossy and cool.

It is cool everywhere. He smells animals. Security.

Blessed.

He smells water. He hears it.

I am blessed.

Two-legged creatures and complexity are gone. Softness remains. He finds the gurgling stream and drinks alone. Then he sleeps, falling into blackness, still alive.

I'm still alive.

An Afterword to this story is on page 253.

18

KLINGER'S PHARMACY

by
Paul D. Scavitto

There weren't many things Tiffany hated, but right now she hated the stinking bearded man in her bed. She stood at the edge of the bedroom, clutching the doorframe. She could feel a sneer clinging to her face and didn't care. She'd spent three weeks taking care of his immobile broken frame, and he dare accused her of lying to him.

Her eyes flickered to the dresser drawer where the divorce paperwork lay hidden under the remainder of her clean socks. For a moment she considered telling him all about it. How she was going to leave *Mr. Going Nowhere Fast*, how she and her sister had planned it all out. The tickets were going to be waiting at the airport for her. She'd even packed two suitcases and a backpack. Thank you, and goodbye. It was going to be so easy, a clean break with the promise of a new start in Santa Cruz.

Her husband gasped and grabbed his shattered left leg. She felt her face soften and shame shot through her. Of the many less than flattering distinctions she could attribute to Simon, having a low tolerance for pain wasn't one of them. The anger began to fade from her mind. He was in pain and maybe even a little delusional.

When the Great Quake, as the scientists called it, had struck he'd been out in the garage working on that stupid '78 El Dorado. That car had been the end for her. They had bills they couldn't pay and he'd dragged home this wreck, shoving it into their garage. Every time she had to drive out in the rain, she was reminded that her garage was filled with that monstrous rusting hulk.

The first quake had been something like a 10 on the Richter scale, whatever that meant, and it had tossed the El Dorado off of the jack like a toy. It had taken her an hour to free him from under the car.

Simon's eyes locked on hers.

"Well?"

She sighed. "Well, what?"

"Where'd you hide my meds?"

She looked longingly at her sock drawer one more time and then turned around leaving the room. It wasn't like there was a court system to process a divorce anyway. She walked out into the clutter of their kitchen.

"WHERE ARE THEY?" He bellowed.

She pulled on her jacket and slid into her boots. The quake had activated all the world's dormant volcanoes and an ash cloud had covered the sky in a thick grey smear. It was cold all the time and there was real fear that all the plants might die, taking the rest of the inhabitants with them.

Before the quake she used to love the cold, but this was different.

This felt permanent.

She waited in the kitchen a moment to see if he would say anything else. He didn't. "I'll be right back," she said. He didn't answer her.

Her father's revolver sat on the kitchen counter and she slid it into her coat pocket. He'd given it to her when she *felt the need* to move west. She hated the thing, but there were packs of dogs and desperate people outside. Not that she'd seen much of either group since the quake. Opening up the door to the house, she stepped outside and over the mud on her doorstep.

The quake had been awful, but what followed had been worse. When the volcanoes had re-awoken, the snow had melted on the mountaintops, causing huge waves of mud and debris to come rushing down, destroying everything the quake had missed. Well, nearly everything.

She looked at the only two other houses in the neighborhood that'd made it through. One had been the home of an elderly couple, the Simpsons. Despite their protests, she had checked on them almost everyday until one day, a few weeks back, no one answered her knock. Mr. Simpson had taken matters into his own hands. She'd searched the place for supplies, but aside from a moldy package of Nilla Wafers, the place was bare.

The other home had a neurotic twenty-something named Jake living in it. He'd started shooting at people who came too near the house, so she kept her distance. She had no idea if he was alive or dead.

She felt her feet settle into the mud. It had solidified some since that first day. If she hadn't known where the road used to be, there'd be no way she could identify it now. The scene in front of her was one of mud-caked ruin. It looked like a giant brown river that had frozen in place. Trapped in this still life torrent were twisted pieces of her neighborhood and bits of shattered trees.

A twig snapped behind her and she froze. She carefully slid her hand into her pocket.

"I have a gun," she warned.

Turning her head in the direction of the noise, she saw a mangy grey dog with three legs. It was wearing a faded green collar and she could see its ribs. It didn't seem interested in her and she suppressed the surge of pity she felt for the poor animal. They barely had enough food to eat as it was.

Pushing the dog from her mind, she clomped along the ruined muddy road. The pharmacy was just a few minutes walk away and it was mostly intact. She'd been making weekly trips there for a while and the shelves were starting to get a little bare. She could see the evidence of her own travels in front of her, giant muddy boot prints back and forth to the pharmacy.

She came to the intersection where Jack's Guns used to be. On the lot where the purveyor of second amendment goods once stood was now part of a mangled steel bridge, probably from somewhere up on the mountain.

Just beyond the bulk of the bridge sat the miraculously untouched Klinger's Pharmacy. "Klinger's, a Pharmacist You Can Trust!" Walking around the giant rusted bulk of the wrecked bridge, she approached the front of the store, scanning it for any changes. She looked at the ground near the entrance to check for any foreign footprints. A moment of panic passed through her.

Is that a different boot print? She strained her eyes, but she couldn't quite make out if it was a separate print or just one she'd made herself.

It's fine. It's just your own print. Go on. Simon needs you to hurry. She stood and looked through the glass door into the gloom of the abandoned store. It appeared to be empty. As she reached for the door, a slight tremble shook the ground. She held her breath. *It's fine.* She waited and it passed.

She pushed open the door and walked into Klinger's. It was only then it occurred to her that she'd forgotten her backpack, which would mean a long walk home with a plastic bag tearing into her hand.

Klinger's was not very large. It had four aisles and the pharmacy counter at the back. Off to the left was a row of four large soda coolers. Prior to the quake she'd never even been inside.

When she kicked the mud off her boots, she saw it as clear as day. A large man's muddy boot prints leading back to the pharmacy counter.

She heard the sound behind her too late. Behind the door, she'd forgot to look behind the *stupid* door. The next thing she knew she was on the ground with a blinding pain shooting through the back of her head. Whoever it was hit her again. For whatever reason the second hit got her moving. She scrambled forward and managed to get her feet under her.

She ran to the end of the center aisle and dove around the corner. Her hand fumbled when she pulled out her gun, and it went skittering down the aisle in front of her. *Stupid, stupid, stupid.*

"No!" she cried.

She felt strong hands on her arms and then she was flying through the air towards the counter. Her head bounced off a watch battery display and she saw little flashes of light. She was momentarily grateful that she was in a pharmacy so she could get some aspirin.

She rolled onto her hands and knees, and could feel blood dripping down her face. Out of the corner of her eye she saw him approaching her. *He's tall and he has my gun.* She whipped herself backward, not thinking, just hoping her instincts would keep her alive. She back-crawled towards the cooler.

"What's your name?" he growled.

She slid sideways along the coolers towards the front door, just trying to put some distance between him and her.

"What is your name?" He pointed the gun at her as he came around the corner. He was standing directly in front of the coolers, no more than five feet away from her. He was well over six feet tall and wearing a filthy set of dark blue Dickies coveralls. It looked like they were covered in grease. He had a wad of chew in his lip and he spit as he was looking at her.

"Tiffany," she answered.

"I never knew a Tiffany. Sounds like a dumb name."

Her mind was racing. He hadn't shot her, so maybe he wasn't going to hurt her. *The door, try to get to the door.*

He crouched down with the gun still pointed at her. "What are you doing in my pharmacy, Tiffany?"

That was when she felt it. It started as a small vibration and then built in intensity until the whole store was shaking around them. Suddenly there was a loud crack and the floor under him gave way and the cooler to his right crashed down on top of him. She could hear his scream as she scrambled back. After a few moments the shaking stopped.

She was wobbly when she stood up and went over to where her assailant was now trapped. He was lying face down on the ground with the cooler on top of his back. It looked like the rest of him was half wedged into a hole in the floor. She grabbed her father's gun back and toed the man in the head. He grunted.

"Puh…please…help…me."

"Why should I? You attacked me!"

He didn't answer her, just grunted and tried to move.

She sighed and put the gun back in her pocket. She got her hands under the edge of the cooler and tried to lift it. She strained for a moment, but there was no way. She couldn't even budge it. He was stuck.

Her mind snapped onto the reason she had come to the pharmacy in the first place. She raced to the back of the store and grabbed a bottle of oxycodone. If she couldn't get him out, the least she could do was make him comfortable. She ran back to where he was and sat on the floor in front of him.

"Open your mouth. I've got something for the pain."

He opened his mouth and she gave him a half dozen of the pills. She grabbed the nearest bottle of soda, and held it so he could drink.

He gasped and said, "Thank you."

She slid down the nearest cooler and sat on the floor next to him. She sat there for a while wondering what she was doing when she blurted out. "What's your name?"

There was a long pause. He shifted and then wheezed out, "Marshal."

"Marshal, why did you attack me?"

Another long pause, and then, "I'm...sorry."

She sat there for a while listening to him struggling to breathe. "Marshal, I can't lift this thing off of you. I tried, but it's too heavy and there's no one who can come help us. What do you want me to do?"

"Mechanic," he grunted.

"What?"

"I was a mechanic...before."

"Oh. I was an accountant. I hated it." She looked at the part of him that was exposed. "What about you?"

He didn't say anything for a while.

"Please...don't leave me...like this. Just...end it."

Her breath froze in her throat. *End it?*

"I...I can't do that," she stammered. "Please don't ask me to do that."

"Just do it," he gasped.

A tear fled from her eye and she wiped it away. She'd never killed anyone. She had pointed the gun at a few people, but that was just to scare them away. She'd never intended to pull the trigger.

She stood up and looked down at him. "I don't think I can shoot."

Suddenly his right hand grabbed her leg and he looked up at her. There was blood coming out of his mouth.

"Please...Tiffany."

She stood there for a long while looking into his eyes. Finally, his strength gave out and he laid his head back on the ground. She shakily pulled the gun from her pocket and pointed it at his head.

She cocked the hammer back.

***

Tiffany switched the plastic bag to the other hand and swore at herself because she forgot her backpack at home. She'd cleared out the painkiller section this time. She didn't know how many more people would find their way to Klinger's.

She squinted her eyes at the brightness of the sun, holding up her free hand to block the light. She'd have to remember to bring her sunglasses next time.

She lowered her hand as realization dawned on her. The sun was peeking through a hole in the clouds. It was beautiful.

She just stood there for a moment and let the sun's rays warm her face. Then she heard something. *Is it music?*

She turned around and listened carefully. It was a birdsong, far away and carried on the wind, but there nonetheless. She listened and it came again fainter this time.

The sun had slid back behind its curtain of ash and she decided it was time to get home. Maybe she would see about building Simon a pair of crutches so he could see the sun.

An Afterword to this story is on page 254.

19

THE APOCALYPTIC DIARIES

by
Stephanie Baskerville

Rations Day. Thank the good Lord because I ran out two days ago. I'm always running out before the next delivery—I can't help it, no matter how much I try. Even reminding myself that *long* gone are the days when I could just go to the grocery store and shop to my heart's content—buying anything I wanted—doesn't help me. Nor do the notes that I write myself.

The original military-issued 1984 HMMWVs make their way down the uneven jagged streets, delivering surplus ration packs, canned goods, and bottled water to those of us who are lucky enough to be alive. Grocery shopping, *any* kind of shopping, is extinct as much as the Timber Wolf.

I stand on the blackened steps of what used to be my beautiful, wrap-around white front porch. Dark volcanic rock, the remnant of the rivers of lava that cascaded through my neighbourhood, makes up a new road. My house is barely

178

recognizable now. No more nice white picket fence—that was destroyed within seconds of the storm that changed my world. No more soft, manicured green grass out front, either. And any wildlife that made its home in my yard is long gone, undoubtedly burned to a crisp, then buried beneath the obsidian flows.

There are no trees anymore. It makes it much easier to hear the sounds of the Humvees as their sixty-year old suspension systems groan over the roughened road they now traverse on a monthly basis. The sound of them approaching draws my neighbour out of his house, the only other survivor in what used to be known as *The Beaches* in Toronto. In a population of over one hundred and thirty thousand people in *The Beaches*, there are now less than fifty of us.

My neighbour sees me watching from my porch and waves to me. I wave back. We had a great relationship before everything went sour. We're trying to find that relationship again, but with the trauma we've been through, it's tough. I do like him, though. I guess that means that my upcoming nuptials to him won't result in *total* misery. Not like my best friend over in Scarborough, who has to marry a man she's barely even met.

But that's what we've sunk to over these past eighteen months. The Toronto Municipal Government literally rules all aspects of our lives now. Big brother, indeed! My best friend wants to find a way to just leave—it'll never happen, though. Not after they micro-chipped every last one of us, ensuring that they can track our every move. Not since they wired our houses with hidden cameras and microphones. There is no escaping this life.

No escaping the fact that the government has taken even our reproductive rights away in an effort to "build up the population" once again. If a woman is of childbearing age and she doesn't willingly unite with the man they assign to her (a parody that they're calling *marriage*), she's arrested and thrown in prison. Women that get arrested don't come out until they're well into their third trimester—artificial insemination, I think.

What happened to democracy? What happened to having rights and freedoms? Let me tell you, all of that flew the coop along with the wild birds around us, who realized before anyone else that something was terribly wrong. Before the earth cracked, fissures burst, and molten lava rained down on us all, destroying everything it touched.

My thoughts are wandering and I pull them back to the present. The Humvees appear, a convoy of six of the gas-guzzling trucks. Always six of them. Soldiers (if they can even be called that) who now form the new *Metro Toronto Forces*, bristle from the vehicles. They hold their fifty-year-old M16s at the ready. Not like they need to. It's just my neighbor and I on the street now. But they're sadistic power hungry scum and they like to pretend they're in control. Truth be told, they're just as much a slave to the Toronto government as we are.

I can't help but watch them with contempt even as I raise my hands above my head in the necessary *unarmed* position. I've known *real* soldiers and this sad excuse for human beings are as alike to my once-heroic friends as a dog is like a shark. All of the men hanging out of the vehicles are sorely out of shape. All of them look slovenly in their uniforms. They're a disgrace, really. But I dare not let them see my contempt—they're the ones with the guns, after all.

Movement out of the corner of my eye catches my attention. My neighbor, thick steel-toed and soled boots looking out of place with his bright Bermuda shorts and white T-shirt, is picking his way across the glassy surface of the obsidian. I'm not sure why he's making his way over. He's supposed to stay on his porch with his hands in the air like mine and wait for them to approach him.

It's clear that the enforcers aren't sure what he's doing, either. I notice a few of them readying their guns.

"Xavier!" I call out, cautioning him. The guns swing around to hone in on me, and my mouth suddenly goes dry with fear. My breath catches in my throat.

My neighbor ignores my warning. However, I notice that he's raised his hands above his head and shifted his direction so that it's clear to the convoy that he has no intention of going near them. He's making a beeline towards my porch. I watch the guns lower slightly and suddenly, I can breathe again. They're not going to give him a hard time.

He reaches my porch.

"Celeste," he says. His melodic voice sends arpeggios up my spine and I restrain a shiver. I'm reminded of the days before the apocalypse, when he and I would sit on this very porch of mine, in the dark, and stargaze. That same voice, speaking out of the darkness, of everything and anything—no topic for us was off limits. Well, no topic except our own relationship. We didn't talk about that. To this day, I'm not sure why.

"Yes?" I ask, bringing myself back to the present again.

"I think we should talk."

"Now?" I look around. "Don't you think this is a rather awkward time for a conversation?"

"I know you ran out of your rations again this month. You didn't even have to come and ask me this time, and I still knew." Xavier's uniquely amethyst eyes are regarding me with a knowing look.

"Yeah, I did," I admit. "I'll be more careful this time."

"Celeste, you don't need to be careful. These guys give out extra rations to married couples and I think it's time we...talked... about that."

I'm confused for a moment. Then I realize what he's saying. My heart leaps, although I'm not sure if it's with fear or with anticipation of what's to come. I realize that, no matter what I say, my life's about to change.

"You want me to tell them that we're married?" I ask. At his nod, my stomach does a somersault. Suddenly terrified, I can barely get the next words out. "We don't have the records to prove it. And they'll ask for those records."

"You have your license, don't you? We can get them to witness us signing it now, and we can get them to report back to the capital that it's been done," Xavier says to me.

He's right. I do have the marriage license that the government issued to me last month in my scorched kitchen. I can visualize it in my mind, sitting on what used to be a beautiful oak dining table. And the government doesn't really care *when* the marriage happens. They scheduled it for next month, but August 22nd, 2042 is their ultimatum date. If I'm married to the man they chose for me before that, so be it.

"Okay," I hear myself saying. "Let's do it."

The soldiers are beginning to unload the crates of rations that will sustain me for the next month.

"Sir?" I call out to one of them.

"What is it?" the man scowls at me.

"Sir, I need a witness for a marriage. I have my license."

"Fine," the man nods. Talking that as permission, I retreat into the interior of my house, barely noticing the sulfuric smell emanating from all around me as I walk through the charred walls. They say you get used to it—I guess I have. I pick the license off the table, find a pen, and hurry back outside.

The men have acknowledged my marriage and have unpacked extra crates for Xavier and me to share. There's over twice as much food and water as I would have normally received. Xavier was right. *Dear Lord, this might just work out after all.*

We are escorted from the porch by two of the soldiers, and Xavier and I sign the marriage license on the hood of the Humvee. The scowling man who is obviously in charge witnesses it and signs his own name below ours. He rips off the bottom copy of the license. This he will register at the capital.

"Celeste Pearson and Xavier Aleksi, I have the pleasure of informing you that you are now considered married in the eyes of the government of Toronto." Sounding exactly the opposite of what he's saying, the scowling man looks about as bored as anyone *could* look. He reaches into the Humvee and pulls out a pouch that jingles with the weight of 50 one-dollar and two-dollar coins. The marriage stipend.

"On behalf of the government of Toronto, I award you your allotted fifty dollars to prepare yourselves for parenthood," he continues. His voice grates on my nerves. "As you both know, you will have six months to prove to the government that procreation has begun. Failure to conform to this will result in imprisonment."

I restrain myself from hitting the man by force of will alone. I try to reason with myself that it wouldn't do me any good. I'd just end up getting myself shot. I can't help but quietly seethe as I watch the man give an ironic salute to both of us. I hand Xavier the stipend, and the man pushes us back towards my porch. Then the man waves to his men to load themselves into the convoy. They do as he commands. Xavier and I watch as the engines roar to life and the convoy jounces its way along the street past Xavier's house.

"I hate them," I mutter, much too low for the microphone hidden in the ceiling of my porch to pick up. Now that I'm married, though, and there is the chance that I will bear children, I've become a source of hope for the government of Toronto. There's no way they'll imprison me now, unless I fail to produce a child within six months. For the first time in eighteen months, since my life was turned upside down, I breathe a sigh of relief that I am, for the most part, safe to at least say what I please.

The feeling is heady like I've drank too much wine. I feel momentarily dizzy, and I sway with the weight that *does* settle on my shoulders. Sure, I've got free reign to say what I want, now. *But what if I don't produce a child within six months?*

At that thought, I begin to shake. An unfamiliar feeling of warmth settles around my shoulders, calming me, and I realize it's Xavier's arm. He's pulling me close to him for a moment. Oddly comforted by this, I sigh inaudibly.

"Well, that's that, then," Xavier says. I can only nod. He looks like he has something else to say, so I wait for him to continue speaking. After a moment or two of silence, he does. "Not quite how I pictured myself getting married."

"Me neither," I have to agree. He looks at me.

"I'm strongly reminiscent of the times when betrothals were arranged every day. But I'm luckier than most of them, at least *I* got to marry a friend."

His words make me look up at him. A half-smile crosses his face as our eyes meet. The expression in his causes my heart to skip a beat, just the way it used to do. I feel my face flushing. Not quite willing to admit the feelings I suddenly experience for Xavier, I turn my head to look at the rations.

"Now what?" I ask.

"We'll have to put those away." Xavier gestures to the pile with his chin.

"Okay. But whose house should we live in?" I'm suddenly overwhelmed by all the things Xavier and I have never talked about, our living arrangements being one of them. *Why should we have?* I quickly ask myself.

"Yours," Xavier doesn't even hesitate. "Both my kitchen floor and the floor in my bedroom are too damaged to support very much weight. I've had to sleep in my living room since the—well, you know."

LAVA STORM IN THE NEIGHBORHOOD

"My floors are stable," I agree, shying away from the end of Xavier's sentence. I don't want to think of the lava. "Most of the damage to my house is cosmetic. Structurally speaking, there's only one hole in my dining room floor."

"I'll pull some of the wood from my house and do some repairs," Xavier assures me. I shrug.

"Alright. Let's get to work, then," I say, then shyly I look up at him. "I'm also glad that I was allowed to marry a friend."

"You're the only thing I have left in this world, Celeste," Xavier says solemnly. I nod.

"Ditto."

Xavier releases me from his arms and we go to work. I'm carrying the first load of ration packs into my—*our*—house when I see movement out of the corner of my eye. Looking up, I am just in time to see a huge raven winging overhead. I'm suddenly filled with optimism.

"Xavier! The wildlife is coming back!" I exclaim. Xavier also looks up. He smiles.

"Guess we're not as alone as we thought," he says, half to himself. My optimism seems to be contagious. Both of us carry on with our work, filled with hope for a better future.

Maybe, just maybe, things are going to work out after all.

* * *

Eight months have passed since I married Xavier Aleksi. I look over at him now, his face taut with worry that he's trying to hide. We *were* lucky. Our marriage blossomed into a deeply loving relationship. But we're not thinking of that right now.

186

We sit in a narrow hallway, waiting for the judge to call us in to the courtroom. We're on trial for murder—our baby's.

Two weeks ago, I miscarried.

An Afterword to this story is on page 255.

20

FLIGHT OF HOPE

by
Glenda Reynolds

When it came to being an entrepreneur, Jimmy Jenkins made it look too easy. He was known for starting successful auto repair shops, selling them, and starting all over again. That in itself is quite an accomplishment. But he didn't stop there. He owned and piloted a private plane in which he made money by flying clients across the country. He had even volunteered his time and money when natural disasters happened such as flying supplies to Haiti or delivering a tanker of gasoline to hurricane Sandy victims. Jimmy does not think of himself as a hero. He has acknowledged that he has been so blessed by the Almighty that he must pay it forward to those in need.

Although Jimmy and his wife Diane were in a financial position to retire, Jimmy found it hard to live the quiet life. There were always more deals to be made and more places to fly. On that note, he agreed to fly clients to Seattle, Washington. Diane's mother who lived in Seattle was having her ninetieth birthday. Naturally Diane wanted to fly out with Jimmy and his client to visit her mother.

It was a beautiful cloudless day when pilot Jimmy Jenkins flew his plane from Atlanta to Seattle. He landed the plane at a private airport that bordered the Mount Rainier State Park. To Diane's delight, Jimmy had reserved a cabin for the two of them near the park. The snow-covered Mount Rainier was picturesque from their little haven.

The blissful night was interrupted by a series of earth tremors, which became increasingly more violent than the ones preceding them. Jimmy turned on the radio in the wee hours of the morning. ABC News was broadcasting a special report saying that reports were coming in from around the globe of various volcanic activities.

Diane was now awake and came out in her robe. *That woman could sleep through anything,* Jimmy thought. She walked into the kitchen to make some coffee. As she filled the coffee maker with water, she looked out of the kitchen window at Mount Rainier. Ash and steam were billowing out from the top of the mountain.

"Holy smokes! Jimmy, come see this." Jimmy was at her side in two seconds.

"Land sakes! Diane, we need to leave as soon as possible. Forget the coffee. We'll have breakfast someplace else far from here."

They dressed and packed in record time. The suitcase was literally thrown in the plane. Jimmy fired up the engine. Soon they were in flight and gaining altitude. While Jimmy concentrated on the instrumentation, Diane gazed at the state park below. Her mouth dropped opened as she saw some of the earth opening up, cabins crumbling apart, and trees falling across the highway; but the worst part was yet to come. The little Cessna Skyhawk continued to climb higher in the sky. More earth could be seen which showed more destruction, similar to where they had just been. The ground looked like it was experiencing a major earthquake as it shook and buckled before their eyes. Large fissures opened in the highways and continued across the valleys and into the mountains. Telephone poles wobbled and collapsed like toothpicks strewn on a table.

There was a brief and eerie moment of silence except for the hum of the engine. Suddenly Mount Rainier exploded open as tons of smoke and ash filled the air. Everything within a ten mile radius was either disintegrated or carried away on the ground by the blast. The wildlife that was not disintegrated was killed by the sulfur dioxide gas. The blast zone extended twenty miles from Mount Rainier, snapping trees in half with a force of twenty-five megatons of TNT.

They were in flight for ten minutes when the cloud of volcanic ash enveloped them and ultimately clogged the plane's engine. The Cessna sputtered as Jimmy tried to find a place to land. There was no highway fit to land on. He saw a good-sized lake that would have to make due. He came about in order to make his approach while backing off the throttle. While the plane skimmed the surface, it hit a bolder, which sent it into several cartwheels before it landed upside down in the water.

Jimmy unfastened his seatbelt and that of Diane's. She wasn't responding. With Diane under one arm, he paddled to the surface and brought her to the shore. She was still unresponsive. After a minute of mouth-to-mouth resuscitation, Diane coughed violently while Jimmy sat her up. A few of the people who lived in the lake homes ran up to them after having witnessed the crash landing.

"Is she going to be alright?" inquired a young twenty-something black woman with long hair.

"I think so. She would've let me know by now if she wasn't. We just need to get ourselves dry and warm if it's possible."

"I'm Bonnie by the way," the woman said as she extended her hand in greeting. "My home has survived both the earthquake and the volcano blast but not without damage. You are welcome to stay with me until we figure a way to get out of here."

"Thank you for your hospitality."

An angry looking man in his thirties was standing outside of his house observing the newcomers. "You better not be feds or else I'm gonna kick your—"

"Back off, Jerod. They are just regular folks in need."

"Well, I *need* for them to stay off my property. I'm sure that looting will be going on big time after this," he said with the sweep of his hand. His black and white pitbull growled at his side.

"Don't worry. I'm sure they aren't interested in your marijuana farm that you're growing. And keep that hell hound away from here!" Jerod gave them all a dirty look and retreated back into his house.

Jimmy stood up and headed back into the water to get supplies from the plane. Bonnie and Diane started to protest. He soon proved that it was a good idea. He brought an inflatable boat, rope, and flares with him. These were stored on Bonnie's fenced property.

Bonnie had been listening to her ham radio of the worldwide earthquake that had occurred. Many reports of inactive volcanoes had suddenly become active at the same time. Thousands of people were either missing or dead. Scientists were already predicting a volcanic winter caused by the ash in the atmosphere that would lower temperatures and last for two to four years. They were already saying that a third of the world's population would die of famine. Many were now in danger of enormous tsunamis caused by the quakes. The entire world was under martial law. Food hoarding would be dealt with forcibly by the police. Looters would be shot on site.

"There is so much chaos," Bonnie exclaimed as she placed her hands on her forehead. "How can they enforce martial law on such a global scale? They couldn't even handle the aftermath of hurricane Katrina here in the states! What makes them think this will be any different?" she asked.

"The fact is, they won't be able to handle it. There are more civilians than there are military or police. I hope you have some sort of gun because we're going to need it," replied Jimmy.

"I have some rifles in a gun cabinet. My dad collected a few. He was employed by the state park many years ago. He taught me how to shoot at an early age which I'm now thankful for." Bonnie opened the gun cabinet to reveal a twenty-two rifle, a shotgun, and a Winchester rifle. Jimmy looked at Bonnie with a new admiration and respect.

"Let's hope that we won't have to use these on people," said Jimmy.

The rest of the evening, Bonnie stayed glued to her ham radio, a hobby handed down by her father. More and more reports were coming in about whole cities that were destroyed by the quake. The fault line from Illinois to Memphis had lengthened to the Gulf Coast. The continental U.S. was now in two separate landmasses. The only way to get back to the East coast was either by plane or by boat. Bonnie continued to turn the dial to pick up radio transmissions closer to home. She came to find out if lahars or volcanic mudflows were making its way out from Mount Rainer. These were caused by the eruption, mixing hot ash with the buildup of ice and snow. It is equivalent to cement running down a cement mixer. The force of the mudslides was strong enough to move mature trees, cars or even buildings. There were a couple of news helicopters that were circling the blast area and reporting the progress of the flow.

"Jimmy, we need to do something before the mudslide makes its way into Seattle. We need to get my mother out of harm's way," Diane implored her husband.

"I know, honey. Let's inflate that raft and take a few supplies. Anyone who wants to come along may do so. We'll get to a highway and try to make it into Seattle."

"I'm coming with you," Bonnie said. "All of the wildlife is dead. My food supply is low. I'd be in a pinch if I didn't come with you."

Just as Jimmy inflated the raft on the shore, he was accosted by Jerod who held a hand gun pointed at Jimmy's head. "I think I'll take that raft off your hands, mister. After all, man's gotta do what a man's gotta do."

Just then, Jerod felt the cold, hard steel of a shotgun in between his shoulder blades. "Are you anxious to meet your Maker, son?" asked Diane. "Just throw that hog leg in the lake like a nice boy." Jerod complied.

Once Diane lowered her gun, Jerod's pitbull stood growling and baring his teeth just a few yards away.

"Get 'em, Spike!" ordered Jerod.

The dog started to attack Diane. A loud boom was heard from the Winchester, which blew a hole through the dog. He somersaulted and stopped in a lifeless heap. Bonnie stepped out of hiding from beyond her fenced property carrying the Winchester. Jerod seethed with anger. All he could do was make vain threats.

"I'll see that you pay for that, Bonnie. I've had it with you. Watch your back."

"Always have," she snickered.

Jimmy, Diane and Bonnie gathered their food and emergency supplies into Hefty bags and placed them in the raft. Two slim tree branches were taken to guide them down the lake since they had no oars. Once they made it to the other end of the lake near the highway, they traveled on foot. They came across a gas station that had recently burned down after the gas tanks ruptured by the quake. An abandoned semi-truck was parked along the road with the keys still in the ignition. Jimmy climbed in the driver's seat while the Diane sat in the passenger's seat. Bonnie sat on a crate in the middle. They could now see at ground level all of the real devastation: dead game animals, homes demolished, and forests leveled. They could see some trees moving and going down which meant that they were seeing the mudslide in action. They needed to speed up and warn people in Seattle. Jimmy accelerated as best he could while dodging crevices in the road as well as other obstructions.

Jimmy drove right to the closest fire station. He told the firemen to alert the public of the oncoming mudslides that would be there in a matter of minutes. The fireman got in their trucks and each took a section of city to call out warnings using megaphones. Volcanic ash fluttered on the streets like gray, dirty snow when vehicles drove by.

Jimmy drove the semi-truck to the retirement home where Diane's mother, Helen, sat on the porch sipping her sweet tea.

"Mama, we came to get you out of the city before those mudslides get here from Mount Rainer."

"Do you mind if I bring some of my friends?"

"Make it quick, Mama. We need to go."

Helen went into the parlor and gathered some of the other seniors for a road trip. They dropped their cards on the table and picked up their canes and walkers. The seniors were helped into the tall trailer to sit on some crates. The arrangement was not comfortable or convenient, yet they were excited to be out on an adventure.

Then just as he thought it couldn't get worse, Jimmy heard on the static sounding radio that Satsop Nuclear Power Plant to the Southwest was very damaged by the earthquake. It was leaking radiation closer to the coast. Minutes later the news anchor stated that the same power plant had just been washed away by a tsunami.

A tsunami? gulped Jimmy. *That would only mean that it would come up into the Puget Sound water way and flood Seattle.* And sure enough, the water started to rise over the banks of the city. As the ocean tried to claim the land it was invading, it swept people and vehicles up and around buildings. It almost resembled a ride in a water park, only this one was deadly. Jimmy tried to steer the semi-truck even though it didn't do any good. The seniors in the trailer were being shaken up pretty bad, but at least they were dry for now. They were being swept out to sea with the strong current of the tsunami. They all stared in horror, afraid of colliding with pieces of buildings and vehicles of all kinds. An occasional person crashed up against the windshield and floated away. Debris from the nuclear power plant could be seen floating nearby.

Hello radiation, Jimmy thought. A giant wave sent the debris crashing into the windshield of the semi-truck. *God, please help me!*

Suddenly Jimmy was jolted awake during the Sunday sermon at First Methodist Church in Atlanta. The minister was preaching from the Book of Revelation. Upon seeing that

196

it was only a dream, Jimmy quietly exclaimed, "Hallelujah!" This got the attention of several church goers as they turned to give him a stern look. He reached over with his arm to hug Diane to himself as he settled in to hear the rest of the sermon.

An Afterword to this story is on page 256.

21

PELE'S WAR

by
Rebecca Lacy

The telltale tingle I get in my nose has never failed me. When I feel it, I know something is about to happen— sometimes it's good, sometimes it's bad. My mother said I had second-sight, and that is why she named me Kamaka, which means 'the eye'. I suppose she didn't think calling me 'the nose' would be dignified enough for *her* daughter. However, it was the lowly nose that saved my children and me.

When I awoke that day, my nose tingled as it never had before, and I knew it was a warning. I stepped outside, and everything was covered with white. The strange substance was cold against my bare feet and squished between my toes. Whatever it was, it was foreign to the Hawaiian rain forest. My nose told me it was important.

I closed my eyes and tried to remember the story my great-grandmother, Mahina, had told me of the white blanket that would cover the earth. What had she called it? Then I remembered: snow. According to legend, there are four sister goddesses that rule the mountains north of Kilauea, and they are rivals of Pele, the goddess of fire and volcanoes. Pele is jealous of the sisters so she had them imprisoned atop of the highest peaks where no one could see them. Mahina warned that the sisters will someday rebel against Pele. When that happens, they will cover the world with snow.

I couldn't remember what she said would happen after that. Would the snow remain? I wracked my brain, grasping at wisps of memory. Slowly, I recalled what had seemed like a fairytale when I heard it as a child: The sisters want to be free, but first they must kill Pele. This would not be easy as long as she remains in her home, Halema'uma'u, which is in the caldera at the summit of Kilauea. So, according to the prophesy, the sisters will lure Pele's young husband, Lohiau, to the top of the mountain, and then cause a mighty storm, and he will freeze to death. In her anger Pele will come out of her caldera to fight the sisters. That is when they plan to kill her so they can finally be free of her tyranny.

I remember asking Mahina, "How will we know when a war is about to begin?"

"You will know, sweet Kamaka, because the air will be freezing and the sky will fall down in white flakes."

My head reeled as I considered this. Could it possibly be true? Could the Earth be about to erupt in war?

I hurried to the twins. If the prophecy was coming true, I needed to figure out some way that I could protect them. With my mate, Hiapo, gone, the responsibility would fall on me alone. He meant well, but his restless soul made it difficult to stay in one place. So now, when we needed him most, I didn't know where he was. In his absence, we would go to Malu, the one my family had always turned to for counsel and encouragement. He would know what we should do.

The three of us scurried down the path to Malu's home where we found him outside studying the snow. He greeted us with his customary good cheer for the children's sake, but I could tell from the look in his eyes that he was worried.

"Go inside children. I think you will find something good to eat. Your mama and I will stay out here and see if we can figure out this white stuff."

Once we were alone, I asked, "Is this the prophesy, Malu?"

"What does your nose tell you?"

"It tells me that danger is imminent."

"I agree with your nose, and I think you must take the children and leave immediately. Go somewhere safe."

"How can I leave? Hiapo won't know where we've gone. I need to wait for him. Surely, he will return soon."

"I'm sorry, Kamaka, there isn't time. You need to go now."

"Where will we go?" I had always lived in the forest. I didn't know anything else. "Come with us. You'll know what to do."

Malu shook his head sadly. "I'm too old and would only slow you down. I will stay and guide others, and send Hiapo to you."

He proceeded to instruct me to take the children and run toward the sea. "When you get there you will find my granddaughter, Ulani, and she will help you."

With a few more instructions, the three of us were once again on our way. Ehehene, true to her name, looked at the entire thing as an adventure and was filled with giggles. Her brother, Aukai, was more sedate and I could tell that he shared my fear, but did not want to frighten his twin.

The snow had stopped by the time we reached the shore, but flashes of lightening and rumbles of thunder announced Pele's growing anger. I wanted desperately to stop and find a place in the rocks for us to sleep, but if the prophecy was coming true, Pele's fury would soon be raining down on us, and there was no time for rest. I had to save Ehehene and Aukai.

Half-blinded by weariness, I stumbled on, trying to remember what Malu had said about finding his granddaughter. Finally, I spotted an outcropping of rock that matched the description he had provided.

Ulani welcomed us into her home, and after eating the meal she had prepared, the children and I succumbed to sweet sleep.

All too soon I felt Ulani shake me and heard her whisper that it was time to leave. "You must hurry. Pele is very angry. Before the lava comes, you must be at sea."

"How can we possibly survive in the sea?" I asked in a voice louder than I intended.

"There is a ship, the *Sea Sprite*, docked nearby. The men who sail her are foreigners and do not know the prophesy. They will be in no hurry to leave until they see the volcanoes are about to erupt. That will give you just enough time to get aboard.

"There is a boy, Pineki, who knows the ship. He will meet you at the shore and guide you. He will help you aboard, and stay with you. He is only a child, but he is capable."

Great! The fate of my family rested in the hands of a child.

"One thing more," she added, "I suppose you realize that your presence aboard the ship will be most unwanted. These are not nice men. Pineki has told me that they wouldn't hesitate to throw a stowaway overboard."

Fear clutched my throat. What horrible fate was I subjecting my children to? If only there had been another way.

The three of us left the safety of Ulani's home with her assurances that she too would soon be leaving. We made our way to the place she told us we would find Pineki. In the distance I could see the Sea Sprite rocking in the water, its masts silhouetted against the night sky.

Shortly, I spotted Pineki. Indeed, he was a tiny peanut of a boy; not much older than the twins. However, even in the darkness, I could see that he possessed wisdom that can only be gained through hardship. The scars he wore told his story better than words ever could.

After minimal introductions, Pineki instructed the twins to climb aboard a piece of driftwood that he had located, explaining that there were men guarding the dock.

"We must approach from the water so's we don't get pinched," he whispered.

With Ehehene and Aukai in place, we pushed the wood away from shore and clung to it as we paddled toward the ship. I grew cold and tired, and I had to will my legs to keep kicking. Just as I was beginning to feel as though I could go no further we reached the dock.

Pineki silently led us to the ropes that secured the ship and showed us how to climb. While we were accustomed to climbing the tree to our nest, the movement of the ropes and the risk of plummeting into the water made this much more challenging. After we had all tried it, he indicated that he would go first and help the children then me over the ship's railing. Once he was aboard, he waved for my son to follow. When Aukai was safely aboard, Ehehene followed. My breath caught in my throat when she slipped. I feared she would fall, but she quickly righted herself and continued on.

Finally it was my turn. I knew it would be more difficult for me, but I didn't realize just how difficult. Inch by inch I worked my way up the rope, my body rubbed raw by the course fibers. Finally, I felt the little hands of all three children reaching out to help me. As I came over the side I lay exhausted at their feet until Pineki urged me on.

"We have to hurry and hide before someone sees us," he warned.

I gathered what little strength I had left and followed him to a small room that was really nothing more than a mouse hole. The entrance was barely large enough for me to fit inside.

"I've hidden here before. We should be safe. 'Course, before it was jus me. It'll be a mite crowdeder with four of us." The generosity exhibited by this waif of a boy caused me to smile in spite of everything.

The gentle rocking of the ship soon lulled us to sleep as I held my children close to me. When we awoke, we could see light shining between the wooden slats. Above us men yelled. I didn't understand their language, but I understood the alarm I heard in their voices as thick ash rained down on them.

I didn't realize how much my fear was written across my face until Aukai took my hand in his to comfort me, and said, "It'll be okay, Mom." I smiled at his bravery and thought how prophetic it was that my mate had named him 'Seafarer.'

The four of us continued to huddle together as we watched the activities on deck. Evidently the sailors understood the peril we were in, and were quickly readying the ship for departure. I could smell their fear every time Pele roared.

Shortly, the ship began pulling away from the dock. The last glimpses I had of Hawaii were of huge rocks pummeling the earth as rivers of lava and fire consumed every plant and building in sight. These were the weapons Pele had unleashed to vanquish her enemies.

As we sailed toward the horizon, I promised the children we would someday return, hoping that it wasn't a lie. We are Hawaiians, and there is no other place on Earth where we belong. Someday, when Pele's anger subsided, surely the Sea Sprite would take us home. If not, then all my children and I would know for the rest of our lives was the tiny hole in the bowels of the ship.

* * *

There was a monotonous rhythm to our life aboard the *Sea Sprite*, and after a while, I lost track of time. So, I really don't know long we were at sea. Occasionally, I considered leaving the ship when we docked in strange lands. I suppose, it was selfish of me to have kept the family on board when we might have had a better life on land. However, I was filled with such a longing to return to Hawaii that I could never bring myself to give up hope. Thus, we remained, adapting to our new life, all the while watching for a sign that we are headed home.

Pineki brought us news and food whenever he dared. The loveable little imp had won the heart of the cook who kept him hidden and threw him scraps of food. The man even saved Pineki's life when another member of the crew discovered the boy. The cook reportedly made a joke about our kind always being on ships, and offered the sailor a dram of rum to divert his attention away from Pineki. When the boy recounted this tale, my blood ran cold to think of that might have happened to him without the kindness the cook had shown him.

Pineki became like a third child to me, as well as my family's lifeline. My children and I would never have survived without him. He told us when it was time to leave one hiding hole and move to another; he taught us how to collect drinking water; how to avoid the cats, and the traps that had been set to ensnare stowaways; and he was always generous with his food. Pineki even took charge of the children and showed them places where they could safely run and play.

One day, he came to our hiding place so excited that he had a difficult time speaking. Finally, he calmed enough to share the news: "We are heading for Hawaii. We'll be there in two days time."

My heart pounded in my chest. We were going home! I was filled with a mixture of excitement and trepidation as I wondered if there would there be any remnants of the once-idyllic land where my family had lived for countless generations.

Ehehene and Aukai had only faint memories of Hawaii. I had done my best to help them remember the magnificent forest, which grew so densely that it was difficult to see the sky. I also told them stories of their father who was brave, handsome, and funny. They could only vaguely remember his features and, to be honest, I too was finding it increasingly difficult to recollect the face that I had known and loved so well.

I told Aukai many times that his father would be jealous of us. Hiapo had always dreamed of being an explorer, and his greatest desire was to travel the seas as our ancestors had. It was his deep affection for the ocean that inspired the naming of our son.

Having seen the fire that engulfed our fair island as we were sailing away, I knew there was little chance that Hiapo, or any of our friends, could have survived. Nevertheless, no matter how unreasonable I knew it to be, I still held a spark of hope in my heart.

During our two years at sea, I had learned the men's language. So, that morning when I heard the one in the crow's nest yell, "Land ho!" my knees grew weak, and I had a lump in my throat. We were home.

Just as we had done when we came aboard the *Sea Sprite*, the four of us waited for the cover of darkness then slipped down the ropes. Suddenly, I knew we had been discovered when I heard a man say, "Hey Jack, look at them crazy rats coming down the stern line. Wanna have some fun with 'em?"

For a moment, we froze until the other responded, "Nah, Let 'em go. They're getting' off the ship not on it."

Once we were safely on land, Pineki stopped. "This is where I leave you."

"Won't you come with us?" I had never considered the possibility that he wouldn't remain with us.

"Thank you, but the *Sea Sprite* is my home…it's the only place I know."

After a tearful good-bye, we went our separate ways, knowing we would never meet again.

The children and I travelled a short way, and stopped at the spot where I thought Ulani's house had been. However, it was completely encased in a thick, ugly layer of lava, and I could only hope that she had escaped.

We walked on, and even in the dark I could see the horrible scars caused by Pele's fury. The lava rocks were sharp, and I wished our kind wore shoes so it would be easier to traverse this new landscape.

Just after dawn I sensed we were in the area where our home had been located. Nothing looked familiar, and I felt tears sting my eyes as I gazed at the evidence of war all around me. However, upon closer inspection, I noticed that there were young palms and other plants growing - promising the forest would someday be as it had been.

Suddenly, my nose began to tingle in that telltale manner it has. Something was about to happen. Before I could even form the hope it would be something good, I heard a familiar sound. I perked up my ears and hushed the children so I could listen. There it was again. Yes, someone had called my name, "Kamaka."

I looked around, straining my eyes in the early light. In the distance I saw a tiny movement in the rocks. Finally, the figure drew close enough for me to see. It was Hiapo. He was alive! Miraculously, we were all together again. We ran to each other with such joy. The children approached him shyly, watching us with eyes filled with wonder. Soon, we were all huddled together, caressing one another's fur as our tails intertwined in an unbreakable embrace. Our family was reunited once again.

An Afterword to this story is on page 257.

22

SILENCE & SONG

by
Angela Drew

"You should eat this."

The edges of the can lid were torn angrily by the cheap, rusted can opener. It's the only one we have, so it's one of our most valued possessions. We need to pass the can carefully as not to tear our flesh on the chewed metal edges.

I shake my head and refuse to reach for the can. The action earns me a smack across the ear.

"You are stronger. You have a better chance. Stop wasting rations on me, you stupid boy."

I press my lips together as I continue to sort though a small pile of scrap metal I collected from various ruins in our town. The hardware store had been directly hit by a fiery rock that had plummeted from the sky. That had started a fire that consumed the entire block—the supermarket, post office, and police station were among the casualties of that fire.

I find a tarnished nail and drop it into my pouch of useable tools.

"Evan, listen to me…"

Plunk. Another nail.

"Evan, please."

Tink. A screw. I can make that work in a pinch.

"Evan. EVAN!"

She does this on bad days, on days when all she can think about is her son breaking from her hold to dash into the chaos of the streets to find his wife. Moments later one of the more powerful aftershocks hit and the buildings lining Main Street collapsed. The street was flooded with panicked civilians searching desperately for loved ones—and they were all buried in flaming rubble. Mrs. Alavaster's son was still buried in that ruin. His wife was probably there too.

I look up at her for the first time since I realized that today would be a bad day. Her eyes are dull and wet. The moisture has poured down her wrinkled skin coating her cheeks and jowls. I want to snap at her and remind her that crying will dehydrate her and I almost died on my last run to the only working well left in town.

But I know I'll just make her depression spiral worse. And while I know, rationally, that she's right—she's an 82-year-old woman who can't help me maintain the house, look for food, or defend our shelter and supplies against other survivors—but the thought of losing her… the thought of being alone in this hell…

If I think too long about it, I'm afraid I'll start screaming and never stop.

I listen to her sob quietly while I work.

Plink. Plunk. Tink.

Sniff.

* * *

There are three houses still standing in Hark's Landing. The survival of the structures can be chalked up to a combination of luck and location. Luck, in that they were not hit by the firestorm of the initial disaster. The volcano that suddenly made itself known had spewed forth rumble and fire as it burst from the once quiet mountains. Flying boulders and molten rock rained down on the small town and destroyed structures with direct hits or with fires that resulted. Location became a factor for those houses that were not initially hit with flying debris and were not close enough to the many infernos that tore through the town. The Alavaster house was a family farm that was set a quarter mile from the closest building. The fires that consumed the town had not reached here. And while a molten glob of rock had destroyed the barn and all the livestock, the two buildings were set far enough apart to prevent the house from catching too.

One of the other two standing buildings is in a similar position to ours. It's an isolated house that sits on the other end of town. I made the trek out to it once and found its owner, an old man named Kerney, was still alive. When I arrived, he was standing on the roof of his house screaming at the sky. I tried to speak to him; he turned his shotgun on me and hit my horse—the only surviving horse from the Alavaster Farm.

I never returned. I don't know if Kerney is alive or dead.

* * *

I lock the garage after carefully sorting the nails and screws into their proper places. The garage is sacred. Tools, weapons, machinery, a bicycle, an ATV—it's my hoard of treasure. It's where I keep the loot I collect from runs into town. There isn't much, and it's precious. After the barn and the silo were destroyed by fire, the garage is the only other standing building besides the house itself. I don't keep everything in the garage; I have essentials stashed in the house too. Watching my town burn taught me to plan for the worst.

I already have wood and soil piled on the roof of the porch. I take a hammer and a pouch of nails with me as I climb to the site of my soon-to-be elevated and protected greenhouse. It will be situated on top of the porch of the farmhouse, protected from everything that the house is protected from, and hopefully, a constant source of food.

With a spare nail between my teeth, I line up the first two-by-four and begin pounding with the hammer.

* * *

The third house... is my old house. It is located in town, but stands amongst the desolation of its former neighborhood. It sustained some damage. It looks like debris crushed the back porch and the former dining room.

I've been there three times.

The first time the building seemed abandoned. I took a few items: photo albums, my father's .22, and my mother's favorite pearl necklace. When I returned to collect more of my family's belongings, the door was nailed shut and "STAY AWAY" was scrawled on it with red permanent marker.

I returned with a crowbar and forced my way in— to find the house untouched… except for four portraits arranged on the mantle over the fireplace. The smiling reproductions of my mother, father and sister were standing in smashed frames and covered in a red substance that looked like paint. I ran my fingers over the shattered glass that separated my callused fingers from my sister's face. I remembered the day the picture was taken. She was laughing and trying to take the camera from me. I snapped the shot while she caught her breath and called me an idiot.

My portrait sat away from the others. The frame was pristine. The glass unbroken. A shrine of dead flowers and small animal bones was built around it. My own face, reflected in the glass of the frame, frowned back at me. My breath cast fog over the image. I began to hyperventilate. I could feel my throat catch and close as a panic attack threatened to set in.

I was startled out of my panicked spiral by a creak of the floorboards upstairs.

Someone was in the house.

I started to sob as I dropped my sister's picture and ran for the front door.

The footsteps were on the stairs now.

I slammed the front door behind me as I clutched at my dirty t-shirt and stumbled towards my bicycle. "STAY

AWAY" was imprinted on my retinas, reflected on everything I looked at as if I'd looked into the sun.

I could hear a wrenching cry coming from the house.

Or it might have come from me.

* * *

My family died in the first fallout. We went on an outing together—shopping for my 17th birthday—and I stayed behind as not to ruin the surprise. They were in Hovey's department store when the building collapsed. I was playing a handheld game and eating potato chips in the front seat of our Volvo.

* * *

I've never been creative at cursing, but my vocabulary exploded colorfully when I saw the state of my to-be vegetable garden.

The boards had been pulled apart. The chewed edges of the wood suggested a crowbar did the work. The nails were bent and unusable. The budding plants were ripped from the soil and salt was poured into the fertilizer.

My knees sank into the soft dirt as I surveyed the wreaked project and cradled my head in my hands.

* * *

I remember sitting in Psychology class, listening to a lecture about memory. I was bored out of my mind—until the teacher started talking about memory and stress. Essentially, stress decreases our ability to recall memories. When I watch, in my mind's eye, the store shake on its mooring and tumble into itself—knowing that my family was inside…I remember the shock. I remember the numbness. And I remember sliding from the backseat into the driver's seat. My parents had left the keys so I could listen to music and run the AC. Later, when I recovered from the mind-numbing shock, I regretted fleeing the scene. I regretted not trying to find them. But I got over it.

They were dead. And risking my life would not change that.

* * *

I have to completely start over on the greenhouse.

This is a devastating setback that I don't share with Mrs. Alavaster as she clicks her tongue at me and moves about the cramped kitchen to make tea. The kitchen used to be a wide, beautiful space, but now we have cans, instant rice, and water jugs piled wherever there is room.

After the fallout, the ash in the sky was devastating. The temperatures have been dropping and nothing is growing. Nothing. I don't know if it's because of the dead vegetation or the initial disaster, but I haven't seen any animals either (aside from the horse that Kerney shot).

I need to build the greenhouse. I need to build a windmill to connect to a generator to run artificial lights.

I kick a dented can of lima beans and it hits Mrs. Alavaster in the ankle. She screams holy hell at me.

I need a way to grow food.

I also need to figure out who sabotaged it in the first place.

* * *

Two weeks straight and I have finally rebuilt the greenhouse. I replaced the soil and built a rickety windmill that will have to do for now. Now comes the part I am not looking forward to. I have a generator for the house, but I need to compartmentalize in case of an emergency. Once I accepted that I need to venture into town to find another generator for my greenhouse, I had to also accept that I knew exactly where to find one.

My father kept one in our basement.

The thought of returning to the house nearly made me spiral into a panic attack. Mrs. Alavaster's wrinkled hand on my arm and her pinched frown brought me back. If I lose it, she certainly will. She hasn't had a bad day in weeks—and I'd like to not shatter the peace, even if it's an illusion.

A few weeks ago I built a cart for hauling larger equipment and materials from town. It latches onto the bicycle I found in the garage. It's crude, but it doesn't require gasoline. I cannot waste gasoline on something as frivolous as transportation.

Mrs. Alavaster is watching from the kitchen window and I wave to her as I peddle to the main road

* * *

The fortifications on the house are even worse this time. I can't think about the person who put them there. I can feel the panic building behind my sternum when I think about the smashed portraits of my family. I know it's probably a survivor like Kerney, someone who lost his mind when civilization crumbed, but that doesn't mean I'm not disturbed by the personal way his madness manifested. I don't want to be shot in the face while breaking into my own house.

I leave my bike a block away and come to the house on foot, slipping through backyards and staying low to the ground. The dry earth crunches under my boots and clings to my knees when I crouch to check that the way is clear. It's odd, despite all of the death, the destruction, the utter chaos of the lava storm…the thing that most unsettles me about its aftermath is the silence. As I kneel before the basement window that I know doesn't latch properly and begin to wiggle it loose, the silence pounds at my eardrums. No hum of car engines. No laughter from the street. Not even the white noise hum of electricity that we were all so accustomed to that we didn't register its presence. No chirping birds. No barking dogs.

Silence.

The window pops open and I grab it quickly to keep it from banging against the frame. I spare one last glance around me and then slip my legs into the basement and slide inside.

I let out a breath I didn't know I was holding when my feet hit the basement floor instead of a pile of something loud and painful. The basement is musty and dark, just as I remember it and I feel warm despite its dampness.

I can see the generator tucked in the corner. It isn't large, just enough to run the essentials during a power outage, but I think it will be enough to run the UV lights I've rigged in the greenhouse.

As I start towards the generator I think about how heavy it is, how bulky. Will it fit on my cart? How will I get it out of the basement? Will it fit in the niche that I built for it in the windmill? I'm excited. Careless.

I don't see the figure in the shadows.

I don't see the crowbar clenched in the figure's hand.

Not until it's too late.

* * *

I avoid being out at night.

There are a lot of rational reasons: I could encounter a crazy survivor, I could get injured falling into a hole or tripping over debris, I could get lost. Those are all good reasons, but the real reason is that nighttime in the new world brings a soul-sucking darkness with it. A darkness so thick, so complete, that it pushes against my eyeballs and pulls the air from my chest. It's devastating. The sun is still able to pierce the ever-present ash clouds and provide dim light, but the moon and the stars can't break through at all.

I've developed many new fears: strangers, fire, earthquakes, starvation…but my new irrational phobia is the dark. I'm terrified of being out in the dark.

And here I am. In the dark.

There's dirt in my mouth and stuck to my face. The pain in my head is almost all encompassing. I can't help but trail my fingers over the back of my head. It's dark and I'm likely concussed, so I'm completely disoriented and sensory deprived. I'm not sure how long I sat there, in the dirt, trying to rearrange my thoughts.

Who am I? → Evan Nedar, 17

Where am I? → Basement of my ruined, former home

When am I? → Night. (I furrow my brow and push myself to do better than that) It's been six weeks since…

What am I? → An idiot.

How am I? → Concussed, bleeding, and possibly about to be murdered.

Okay. Time to get up.

* * *

It turns out, I needn't be afraid of the dark tonight.

That realization brought me little solace when I processed why. I crawled from the basement to the street and I saw a light so bright and unlikely I almost thought I was, in fact, dead. But in the flickering of the light I made out the shape of my windmill and my heart crawled into my esophagus when I recognized the Alavaster Farm in the distance.

On fire.

* * *

I don't remember the bike ride back to the farm, but I know it must have happened. It was either my brain sputtering in and out of rationality due to the damage to the back of my skull or the pressing fear of the dark or the choking dread of the fire.

I dropped the bike by the giant oak tree in front of the house and ran up the creaking steps of the farmhouse. Flames had completely consumed the second floor and the windmill.

The moment I pushed through the front door and into the kitchen, I was hit with a wave of heat so intense that I flashed back to the first lava storm. The hurtling rocks, the collapsing buildings, the city blocks consumed with flames—and the memories choked me nearly as effectively as the smoke filling the cluttered kitchen.

Mrs. Alavaster was sitting at the kitchen table; a teacup was perched between her wizened fingers. She looked unconcerned that the house was coming down around her. For an insane moment I thought: *Oh, she's having a bad day today.*

"I thought you weren't coming back, Evan." She didn't look up from her tea.

A stupid giggle boiled up within me at the thought that the tea might be cold.

"I thought that you left me," she said.

"I didn't," I try to say, but I'm coughing too much and a wave of dizziness hits me.

I stumble across the kitchen and try to help her up. She looks at me with an odd frown.

"You're bleeding."

"Yeah," I mutter in her ear while trying to lift her up, "I fell."

"Oh. She said that she hit you rather hard with a steel pipe."

I let go of her as if she were on fire and then stumbled and fell as I noticed what I know had not been there before—

A woman sat in the chair across from Mrs. Alavaster. Her hair hung in clumps around her shoulders. She was dressed in rags, one of which was wrapped around her face, presumably to filter the smoke, possibility to hide her face.

"Hello, Evan," she said.

"I—I…"

"Have you forgotten me so quickly? That doesn't surprise me. Not really."

I could hear something collapse through the ceiling towards the back of the house, but everything seemed to be muted, like I was hearing and seeing through a cloth wrapped over my ears and eyes.

"You left me to die, after all. Why should I expect you to think of me?"

I opened my mouth to ask what she was talking about, who she was, if this was a dream, but nothing came out. I was silent.

"I knew. I knew you had forgotten me, but I have not forgotten you. All I have thought of is you."

Creases formed around her eyes as if she were smiling. Mrs. Alavaster petted me on the top of my head. She got blood on her fingers.

"Dear, I don't know why you didn't bring her home sooner. She's such a nice girl." Mrs. Alavaster clicked her tongue at me and smiled at the woman across the table.

The woman didn't take her eyes off me as she reached up and pulled off the rag. The world slowed and my heart might have stopped when I saw her face.

I'm not sure why I didn't recognize her eyes. Maybe because they have turned cold, colder than I ever knew them to be. Certainly not the carefree warmth I remember from the picture smashed and spattered with paint on my family's old mantle.

"Samantha."

She smiled; a cold grimace at the note of awe and agony in my voice.

My sister. My sister was alive.

She stood then. I could see that she still had the bloody pipe in her hand from the basement.

"I watched you, you know." Her eyes were on me as she paced the kitchen, unconcerned at the fire popping and clawing at the hundred-and-twenty-year-old timber surrounding her.

"The building—the building collapsed. You and mom and dad...you were in there."

That tight smile again. "I was coming out to ask you something. I was hit by flying bricks, but I came to in time to watch you tearing out of the parking lot."

I could see her cold façade cracking.

"You left us there," she whispered. "You left me to die."

"Sam—" was all I was able to get out before the pipe connected with my temple and everything went dark again.

* * *

"You should eat this."

Mrs. Alavaster holds out a can of tuna fish. The ashes of the burned out farmhouse are still smoldering as the truck is packed. Mrs. Alavaster sits in the passenger seat poking at the pink meat in the can.

"Don't cut yourself."

"Oh, you sound just like Evan. Where is that stupid boy, anyway?"

The young woman plucks a pair of sunglasses off the dashboard and smile at her, "I don't know. I'm not my brother's keeper."

The old woman clicks her tongue at Samantha as she turns the key in the ignition.

"Oh, look!" Mrs. Alavaster nearly drops the precious can of food as she points out the window of the truck. "It's a thrush! Can you hear its song?"

A small bird is perched on a broken bit of barbed wire fence at the end of the driveway. Its song pierces the silence as the truck comes to a stop and the crunch of its tires ceases.

"Yes," I said. "I can hear it."

An Afterword to this story is on page 258.

23

THE ADVENTURES OF
SAWYER THOMAS

by
Robert Tozer

The edge of the sidewalk broke off and a huge section of the street simply floated off like an ice floe that had broken away from a marine ice field in the Antarctic Ocean.

A woman in her late thirties, along with many others from her neighborhood, could do nothing but watch helplessly as they were swept away from the mainland. Suddenly, the swiftly moving landmass began to crack and erode. There was fear in the woman's eyes and she flung out her arm and shouted something. Her voice was lost in the hissing, crumbling noise of the sinking mass that used to be the street upon which she lived. The woman looked around but had nowhere to run to, and so she simply stood there and waited for her end.

The lava finally melted the street into an unstable platform, and one end of it rose up precariously and tipped backward. And then she was gone, swallowed by the orangey-redness of living earth.

"MOM!"

Sawyer awoke in a panicked sweat. His breathing was so quick and shallow that he felt lightheaded, and he gasped and wheezed, unable to catch his breath. His heart threatened to pound out of his chest and a roaring sound, not unlike a river cresting over a waterfall, filled his ears. He bolted upright in bed and his eyes darted around the darkened room. When he finally registered that he was at home in his bedroom, his heart sank but his breathing began to return to normal. His head dropped back into the softness of his pillow. And even though his sheets were soaked with sweat and felt mighty uncomfortable against his skin, he continued to lay there until his body had shaken off the nightmare and he felt more like himself.

While growing up, his father's favorite book had been Mark Twain's illustrious, *THE ADVENTURES OF TOM SAWYER*, and he'd decided to encumber his son with its namesake.

"Gee, thanks, Dad. Like I don't get teased enough already in school."

His middle name was equally as bad—Thomas. *Well it could've been worse. I could've been named after Twain's other famous novel, THE ADVENTURES OF HUCKLEBERRY FINN.*

"Huckleberry," he said aloud, and shuddered at the prospect.

Sawyer maneuvered himself out of bed and made his way to the window. He drew open the blinds and looked outside. *Yep. Just like it was yesterday.*

The lava had remained a river and continued to flow down his street and effectively cut the block in half. His gaze followed the street of lava and he saw that it emptied into what looked like a large lava lake at the end of the block. His home was the last house on a dead end street. Only three houses had remained untouched by the burning hell from outside; his, his neighbor's directly beside him, and the house down the street belonging to *Russell Bailey.*

Russell Bailey was the neighborhood bully, and not just in the physical sense of the word either. He had a distasteful way of getting at your feelings with words as well.

He'd seen Russell from his window yesterday. Russell had been quite busy throwing sticks into the lava river and laughing when they'd catch on fire. Sawyer could easily picture Russell throwing kittens in the liquid earth and enjoying it just as much, if not more. Russell wasn't outside at the moment and Sawyer thought that this would be a good time for him to go out. He hadn't been out since before the earthquakes and the consequent upheaval of lava. He hadn't been out since he lost his mom to the red river. Sawyer wiped away his tears and promised himself that, today, he would make it outside.

Sawyer sat at the top of the landing. He readied himself, and now all that remained was to travel down the stairs. But he grew doubtful as he looked down the winding staircase. He was more than a little scared. *That's a long way down.* Nevertheless, he shook his head and resolved to put his body into action. He grabbed his left leg and dropped it off of the footrest, and then did the same with his right leg. He squirmed his rear-end around until he bordered the edge of the seat. In his calculations he didn't factor in the possibility of his wheelchair tipping over, and he found himself tumbling down the stairs in a pain filled ride. Once at the bottom, he groaned, and felt a large knot growing on his forehead. He swore. It was only the "S" word but it would still have consequences if his mom had overheard him. *Oh, yeah.* A new round of tears welled up in his eyes. He sniffled and fought to hold them at bay.

He escaped from the stairs without further incident, and then crawled over to *Red Bullet.*

Red Bullet was a super sleek, motorized, special edition wheelchair from the Hot Pursuit wheelchair company. It had all the modern conveniences—luxuriously thick leather padding, a stereo CD player, a cup holder, a digital dashboard, and a super cool feather-touch button, fifteen-inch, blue-lit LCD command screen. He had literally drooled the first time he'd seen it.

Now safe in Red Bullet, he headed out the front door. The battery icon on the dashboard showed he had a full charge. That would give him about ten hours of use, twelve, if he didn't push her too hard. After that Red Bullet would become Red *Dead-Weight.* He cruised along to his neighbor's house. He didn't know their name because they had moved in just two weeks prior to the disaster. Once, he thought he'd seen a kid go up the driveway, but it could've been the paperboy for all he knew. Red Bullet came to a whisper stop, and Sawyer looked at the upper windows of the house. He scanned farther down the street, and kept a watchful eye out for Russell Bailey. Not seeing any sign of the bully, he took a chance and called out in a loud voice, "Is anybody there? Anybody?" He heard someone call out and then what sounded like someone crashing down the stairs. The front door opened a crack, and a kid peered out. *It has to be a kid. Only half of his head is visible, and he's hiding behind the door and won't come out.* Sawyer encouraged Red Bullet to move along the grass and up to the front stoop of the house. "Hey," he said, "what are you doin' hiding like that?"

The kid returned, "I just am, is all. My parents told me I can't open the door to strangers."

"Well, what's your name then?"

"Ricky."

"Well, Ricky, I'm Sawyer. So I guess we're not strangers anymore, are we?"

Ricky thought for a moment, and then opened his door wide and stepped out onto the porch. "I guess you're right."

Sawyer could see that there was something wrong with Ricky. He was slow, well actually he was retarded, but mom had always said that it was rude to call them that. He didn't understand it, but as he looked over Ricky he understood that he would be heeding his mom's advice. Ricky was a giant; well, a giant for a kid, anyway. He was tall; at least head and shoulders over Sawyer. He had thick powerful arms and legs, and a big barrel-like chest.

"Where are your parents?" Sawyer asked.

"They're just gone. They went away awhile ago and didn't come back. I must have made them mad."

Sawyer knew that Ricky's parents were never going to come back...just like his mom.

How about we go have a look around?" Sawyer asked.

"Outside? I'm not allowed to go outside by myself!"

"But you won't *be* by yourself, you'll be with me," Sawyer said cheerfully. He would never admit it to anyone, but he was lonely. And besides, Ricky seemed nice enough.

Ricky paused a moment, his facial features churned something awful while he thought. He finally wrestled the answer out of his head and into his mouth. "I guess you're right."

Ricky turned and quickly disappeared into his house. He returned a minute later, and adjusted the straps on a helmet that looked something like his Uncle Dave's motorcycle helmet.

Sawyer couldn't help but ask, "What in the world are you wearing?"

"It's my helmet."

"I can see that, but why are you wearing it?"

"I always have to wear it when I go outside. It's in case I fall down and hurt myself. One time I went outside and forgot it, and I tripped and got my head all blooded on the ground. I have to wear it when I go outside. Don't you have a helmet?"

Sawyer shook his head. "I can't walk so I don't really need one." He absently touched the bump on his forehead. *Woulda come in handy earlier though.*

"You mean you legs don't go?" Ricky asked.

Without receiving a reply, and having suitably adjusted his helmet to a comfortable position, Ricky bounded down the stairs of the porch taking the steps two at a time in a reckless, carefree manner, and then dashed over to see Sawyer. He bumped into Red Bullet in his effort to stop, and then caressed one of the handles and the side mirror. "I really like your car! Can I have a turn ridin' it next?"

Sawyer shook his head but was careful to speak nicely to Ricky. "It's not a car. And her name is Red Bullet. I won't be able to get around if I get out of her."

Ricky's resultant frown, complete with lower lip pout, made Sawyer feel terrible, and he said with a sigh, "Maybe later, okay, Ricky?"

That seemed to satisfy Ricky and he excitedly said, "I promise to bring it right back when it's my turn. I won't even get it blooded or anything!"

"Come on, then," Sawyer said. "Let's see if we can make it down to the mall and see if anybody else is around."

They traveled together to where the main road should have been and Sawyer saw that the lava lake was just that—an honest to goodness, real sized lake, only it was comprised of lava and not water. He saw land on the other side but couldn't make out if other survivors were there.

Suddenly, a nasally unpleasant voice barked from behind them. "Well, if ain't the retard and the crip. What are you two turds doin' out here?"

Without turning around to face the voice, Sawyer closed his eyes, raised his head as if in prayer, and then quietly sighed out the "S" word. He knew that the scratching on chalkboard voice belonged to none other than, "*Russell Bailey*." He'd spat the name out with bitterness.

"My name is Ricky," he politely said.

"My name is Ricky," Russell Bailey mocked in a disturbing, half-witted imitation of Ricky. "You didn't answer my question, dummy; what are you two losers doing out here?"

Sawyer spun Red Bullet to face the bully and challenged him. "You cut that out, Russell Bailey."

"Or what, Robochair? You gonna run me over with that rusted tin can?" Russell sauntered up to the pair and knocked on Ricky's helmet. "Hey! Anybody home in there?" Ricky just stood and smiled absently at him. "Thought not," Russell said with a smirk. Then he moved his face close to Ricky's, laughed callously, and said, "Nice helmet, spaz!"

"Thanks," Rickey returned. "Did you lose your helmet? 'Cause if you did, I have an extra one. It's blue! You could use it. I'll let you and all."

Russell shook his head and directed his comment to Sawyer. "No one has answered my question yet. I thought you were broken not stupid."

"We're trying to see if there are any other survivors, and if we can make it out of here," Sawyer said matter-of-factly. "We're eventually going to run out of food and fresh water, and it would be nice to get to a safe place, don't you think?"

"Well, for your information, I was looking through my father's binoculars and saw people on the other side of Lake Melts A Lot here. But since the road's not here anymore, the only way to get there is by going around." Russell changed his voice to mimic that of a robot. "But I think that Iron Weiner here will have an impossible time getting over *that*." He pointed toward the mountain that sat at the edge of town, and which now seemed to be holding the lava at bay.

Sawyer looked up at the mountain and thought that it would be a tough hike for a normal person to accomplish, let alone for the pair of them, handicapped as they were.

Russell cruelly laughed when he saw Sawyer's look of defeat. He suddenly pounced forward, and knocked Red Bullet over which caused Sawyer to plunge to the ground.

"Hey, don't hurt my friend!" Ricky shouted.

"Or what? You'll stupid me to death? Ha Ha! I kill myself! See you lamebrains later." Russell began to walk away, but then he stopped and turned around to warn the pair. "And you two yo-yos better stay away from my house in the future. If I catch you around here again, I'll do more than just introduce you to the grass. Got me?"

From the ground, Sawyer gave him a nasty look while Ricky lifted Red Bullet upright. Ricky began to help Sawyer up but Sawyer roughly pushed Ricky's hand away and said angrily, "I can do it myself!"

Ricky's feelings were hurt and he cried loudly as he ran back home.

Out came that "S" word again. His mom would've had a fit. This was the third time today, and that would've earned him a bar of soap in the mouth. He moved his tongue around the inside of his mouth and reminisced over the awful taste. Then with great difficulty, he finally managed to make it back up onto Red Bullet. He manipulated the directional control and got Red Bullet up to her top speed of ten miles per hour and drove to Ricky's house. He arrived at the front porch and called out to Ricky. "Hey! Look, I'm sorry. I didn't mean to hurt your feelings." There wasn't a reply, but Sawyer noticed the curtains in the front room part. Ricky peered out, and sunlight reflected diamond-like off of the metallic silver paint of his helmet. "Ricky, I *am* really sorry. I was just mad at that stupid Russell Bailey." Sawyer lowered his voice and spoke sadly to himself. "And at myself for being so useless." Ricky opened the curtains wider so that he could fully be seen, but continued with his silence. "Come on, Ricky. Did you know that I've never let anyone else ride Red Bullet before? But, I'll make an exception for a really good friend." He paused, but Ricky only looked back at him with a confused expression. So Sawyer opted for the direct route. "Ricky, I believe it's your turn to drive my car."

Ricky disappeared from the window, and seconds later, threw open the front door. "You mean it?! Really?!"

"Really," Sawyer said with a smile. "But only if you'll help me get out and then get back in again."

"Sure! I like to help friends," said Ricky excitedly.

Ricky got his ride, and only made Sawyer wince once when he almost ran Red Bullet into a telephone pole.

When Sawyer was back in the driver's seat again, he asked Ricky, "Do you think we could make it over that mountain together? We really have to find somewhere safe to go. Maybe your parents are over there." Sawyer hated to lie, but for Ricky's own good he had to be convinced.

"But what about my room?" Ricky voiced in a worried tone. "How can we take it with us?"

"We'll have to leave that behind; same goes for Red Bullet here. We *have* to go Ricky. This is important."

Ricky's eyes welled up with tears at the prospect of leaving his new, but familiar, surroundings behind. "I just got used to my new room…but I guess so, if it's important to my friend."

"It is, Ricky. Do you think that you'll be able to carry me? The main part of town is a long way from here."

"I'm strong, Sawyer! My mommy says that I'm too strong sometimes and I have to be careful."

"Ok. We'll have to take some supplies with us. Do you have any food here?"

"Yes!" Ricky said excitedly. "There's a big jar of animal crackers on top of the fridge. But I'm only allowed to have three a day."

"That's good, but do you have any real food?"

"Animal crackers are real food, Sawyer," Ricky said in all seriousness, "you can touch 'em and everything; they're not real animals though, just cookies."

"You'll have to carry me into the kitchen so I can see what you have. My mom was on her way to the grocery store when the earthquakes happened, so I don't have much in the way of food."

Ricky carried Sawyer in and sat him down on a kitchen chair. He located an empty knapsack, and then began to fill it with the supplies that Sawyer directed him to.

Once they were sufficiently prepared, Ricky carried Sawyer out to Red Bullet again. They travelled back to the lava lake at the end of the street, and Sawyer breathed a sigh of relief when he saw that Russell was nowhere in sight. He stared up at the imposing mountain, and thought that it had actually grown larger since they'd last seen it mere hours ago. After whispering an affectionate farewell to Red Bullet, he turned to Ricky and said, "Well. Here we go. It looks as if our adventures have only just begun!"

An Afterword to this story is on page 259.

1
AFTERWORD

by
Randy Dutton

author of

THE MUDPOT

I live on the 'Ring of Fire' in western Washington. It's a beautiful, life abundant area, but we are in constant threat of the 'Big One', a massive earthquake that can trigger a towering tsunami and explosive volcanic eruptions. Survival depends upon preparation and cooperation. That begs the questions, how many survivors will cooperate and who will become bullies?

2
AFTERWORD

by
Shae Hamrick

author of

EMBERS FOR AMBER

After learning of the premise for Lava Storm, I settled on the idea of a family who had survived an event similar to Mount Saint Helens explosion. My geology class studies were a little fuzzy so I did some research on the different types of volcanic eruptions and aftermaths. Using that I then chose a young girl as my POV as I imagined struggling after all this would be most difficult for her. I then gave her a hard-nosed brother and supportive father, then set them off to find out how to get to safety and who all survived. Along the way, I thought it would be neat if they ran into a questionable character but not someone they would have known, so I made him a hunter. It was fun figuring out how it would all come about and I hope you enjoyed the story.

3 AFTERWORD

by
Mike Boggia

author of

MY BROTHER'S KEEPER?

My Brother's Keeper? sprang from winters spent in the Catskill Mountains, growing up on the family farm. I loved hiking through snowstorms and navigating a large area of swampy ground around the spring fed pond. The ground never froze solid. One misstep and it was up to your knees in mud. Many days Mom scolded me for coming home with toes white and numb. The thought of how a person would react if they found someone they feared, loathed, or hated, who was lost and hypothermic, passed through my mind. What would you do?

4
AFTERWORD

by
Sharon Willet

author of

WE CAN'T FEED THEM

I've found if I wait until suppertime I can go outside without fear of the neighbor's dogs. That much of the story is true and the fact that more and more are stockpiling for a plethora of reasons. I only wish I had a basement full of supplies. Another truth found in this story is the difference in how Dean and Eleanor see the world before them. If we were suddenly thrown into a world such as this, which one of the characters would you parallel? I feel blessed to have a part in this compilation.

5
AFTERWORD

by
Susan Davis

author of

IN THE LIGHT OF A QUAKE

Addison and Zane would always remember their honeymoon experience, which gave them a deep insight into life after an apocalypse. Maybe it wasn't a full-fledged ending of the world, but it managed to change their outlook on all life forever. They've dedicated their lives to survival, and now own and operate *Survival for Life*, a commune-retreat capable of sustaining life for any undetermined length of time.

6
AFTERWORD

by
Laura Stafford

author of

FAIR MEADOW ESTATES

Like unpredictable Mother Nature, how humans react to unforeseen events is always interesting. In *Fair Meadows Estates*, I wanted to experiment with the defiant couple - what could happen to the people who opt to stay behind? In every natural disaster, there's always that one family, that one person, that one couple who refuses to leave everything they've worked for, who believe they can *weather the storm*.

This story is about that couple. Not only do they have to contend with a natural disaster - finding supplies, keeping their wits together and just surviving - this couple also has to deal with a psycho neighbor.

Writing this story, I wanted to find out what would happen to this couple - how would they react? What would they do? Would they panic? Would they finally evacuate? How would you respond?

7
AFTERWORD

by
Lynette White

author of

THE INCOMPARABLE
ANGIE WILLIAMS

In a world that becomes increasingly smaller by the moment, we witness disasters as they are happening. It is in those moments we gasp, cry, feel helpless, cheer, and even scream in rage. But there are those who boldly race toward the danger knowing full well what they face. Where would our world be without our heroes?

Angie Williams encompasses many facets of human nature. When I created this story I wanted to focus on the unconquerable human spirit. Hopefully you find a little bit of Angie in yourself as you read this story.

8
AFTERWORD

by
Harry Alexiou

author of

A BROTHER'S LOVE

This is a story of a young man who is unexpectedly thrust into the role of a parent, responsible for keeping his young brother safe and keeping positive through a difficult time. Pete has to assume the role whilst battling with his own feelings of loss. At times we see the character reduced to tears knowing that he will probably never see his parents again but he is adamant his young brother, Luke, will not see his pain; instead he attempts to keep the child busy with activities and deflect difficult questions…something all parents should be accustomed to. The parent figure of Pete is seen to prepare for a violent reaction to protect his brother when Marvin is close to smashing the window. This is an instinctive response which any parent or guardian would feel in the same situation…to stand up and protect our loved ones.

9
AFTERWORD

by
Randall Lemon

author of

MERCY KILLING

It's not always easy growing up with a brother or sister. They call it sibling rivalry and it is documented throughout history. Cleopatra despised her brother, Ptolemy XIII and her sister, Arsinoe IV which ultimately resulted in the death of Cleo's siblings. Even going way back in the Bible we hear the story of Cain's murder of his brother, Abel.

Though many of us love our siblings dearly we often argue and fight with them. Obviously this situation brings some stress all its own. How much worse can this stress become when acted upon by outside forces? How fragile is the bond between brother and brother when the entire world is in chaos? Can it endure or will it result in death or worse?

In this story, *Mercy Killing*, written for the Neighborhood Anthology, two brothers, Hank and Freddie, who have never gotten along approach a crisis point in their relationship as they put that old saying, *blood is thicker than water*, to the test.

10
AFTERWORD

by
Christian W. Freed

author of

THE LAST DAWN

I've always preferred lengthy novels over short stories, but couldn't pass this opportunity up. The inspiration for the Last Dawn came from the strange combination of disaster movies and the hubbub over the Mayan prediction that the world would end in 2012. (Whoops) I tried to show the hardships of life as well as the internal struggle of the main character with one of his family. After all, we all have black dogs. Break down the laws and we'll see how it plays out.

11
AFTERWORD

by
H.M. Schuldt

author of

DRAGONSHIP

When Miss Margaret and her new young friend, Lily, are stuck on an island that is slowly crumbling away, Lily never gives up that they will get off the island. I worked with the theme, My Brother's Keeper, by having Margaret make an effort to watch over Lily.

With the hope of seeing a ship off in the distance, the survivors soon realize that they have to build a boat in order to sail out. I began to wonder how many people actually know how to build a longboat or would attempt to build one without being able to refer to the Internet. What if the only way to survive was to build a boat and set sail?

In *Dragonship*, there are three boats for two hundred people. Can the people survive long enough while the boats are being built? Tension rises when the three main leaders, Roger, Elton, and Ferrell, do not get along and one of them bullies Norma the cook, wanting to take away provisions from the others. What happens on the island, stays on the island.

12
AFTERWORD

by
Joyce Shaughnessy

author of

A DEMON UNLEASHED

My previous experience before *A Demon Unleashed* was historical fiction. When I found a wonderfully talented group of fiction writers, I had a chance to come out of my comfort zone. This short story was an eye opening experience for me. I found the monthly contest gave me a wonderful chance to stretch my writing abilities in difference genres. I have a great deal of respect for all of the writers in the group and have enjoyed my time with them.

13
AFTERWORD

by
Sylvia Stein

author of

WHEN THE DUST CLEARED

This is a story about a woman named Nadia Chumsky as she is experiencing a chaotic turn of events. She is narrating her own journey. She shares her memories and the love of her one time love. This is a story of how we must love those around us and never take anything for granted. When I wrote this story I wanted to show how life is precious and to try to live each day to the fullest.

14
AFTERWORD

by
Janet Bond

author of

BY THE HAND OF GOD

I wrote *By the Hand of God* to show how people can stick together in times of trouble. The world can end in a split second if God wanted it to. Janet was the main person because she was strong and calm. She said a prayer and believed in what she prayed about. She made sure that her oldest neighbor, Mrs. Mary, was safe.

Janet stood up to a bully who always made trouble for the neighborhood. In the end he didn't make it through the storm because of the way he treated people. Janet opened up her home to everybody, and they all pitched in to do what they could to help each other. In the end they were saved because of their faith and because they gave thanks to God.

15
AFTERWORD

by
Douglas G. Clarke

author of

LIVING IN THE SHADOWS

When writing *Living In The Shadows*, I wanted to take a different look at the typical end-of-the-world story. Here is a family that was spared from a disaster that destroyed their town and they use that as a sign that they should bless others because they have been blessed. Through the course of the story, I wanted to show the ebbs and flow of faith: looking for food, running to the cellar, but still knowing that things were going to be okay. Henry, Beth and Jake are the kind of family I hope mine would be.

16
AFTERWORD

by
Gail Harkins

author of

THE UNWELCOME GUEST

Who killed Lem Bastardi? There are plenty of suspects. It could have been Laurel, taking revenge for her beloved, cat. Uncle Todd could have decided remove a threat to the security of the rural community. Or, a cougar could have made the first blow. Perhaps it was a combination, or something else entirely.

The story of what happens in the aftermath of devastation touches on the dangers individuals face when the usual rules break down and survival depends upon fending for yourself and protecting those around you. How long will you turn the other cheek? Where is your breaking point? When you take a stand, what will that stand be? It's not something most of us have to think about routinely or, if we're fortunate, ever.

I hope you enjoy this tale, and the other takes of disaster in this collection!

17
AFTERWORD

by
Amos Parker

author of

THE WILD REMAINS

This was one of the very first stories I wrote for Professor Limn. I tried to be a little more poetic than usual. Not sure how it comes off to others. But I often like thinking about the non-human life of the world, and how marginalized it gets by humanity. So in this story, while a worldly disaster marginalizes even humanity, the tables turn a little. Also, what would happen if other worldly life (like wolves) had millions of years to evolve? Would they become sentient, like us? And are we denying other life a chance to grow, by wiping out so much of it? And does the larger world even care, either way? Or does the *earth abide*, as the title of the classic George Stewart world disaster fiction book imply?

18
AFTERWORD

by
Paul D. Scavitto

author of

KLINGER'S PHARMACY

The post-apocalyptic world is a fun place to write in, but the post-apocalypse itself is never as interesting to me as the characters that are trying to make their way through their ruined world. In Klinger's Pharmacy I was attempting to take characters with real world problems and set them against the backdrop of the fantastic. This story also ends with something of a question for the reader to consider. Did she or didn't she? I have my own theories, but ultimately that's up to you.

19
AFTERWORD

by
Stephanie Baskerville

author of

THE APOCALYPTIC DIARIES

Apocalyptic literature is, for me, a chance for us to get a glimpse of *what could be*, depending on the choices that we make in our lives. A warning, sometimes. I wanted to challenge myself with *The Apocalyptic Diaries*. Not only was it a short story, which I haven't been very successful at writing before (my shortest ever was forty pages…), but also getting to write a first-person, dystopian society-type story to boot. I loved that challenge, and after countless revisions, including a new ending (courtesy of my husband, who said the last one was *not gritty enough*), *The Apocalyptic Diaries* emerged.

20
AFTERWORD

by
Glenda Reynolds

author of

FLIGHT OF HOPE

Flight of Hope was a real challenge for me in that writing about the destruction of earth, at least on a biblical scale, is hopeless and depressing. In real life cases it isn't about *if*, but *when* regarding natural disasters. When I planned to do the surprise ending, it was then that I could finish writing the story. This is a story about surviving what life throws at you albeit on a grand scale. The main characters were based on the life of a real entrepreneur/pilot and his wife; although, I gave them fictitious names.

21
AFTERWORD

by
Rebecca Lacy

author of

PELE'S WAR

When I read about a natural disaster, I always wonder about how wildlife has been affected. They don't have the Red Cross to help them out. There is no evacuation ship ready to transport the tiny creatures out of harm's way. That is why I wanted to explore the lava storm concept from the perspective of a mother rat.

As for Pele: I would like to say that I learned about her on my visits to Hawaii, but I didn't. Nope, I owe that to the Tiki Room at Disneyland!

I hope you enjoy reading *Pele's War* as much as I did writing it.

22
AFTERWORD

by
Angela Drew

author of

SILENCE & SONG

My uncle died in a fire when I was eighteen. It took almost a week to find his body. The most crushing revelation for me was that he was found in a stairwell. He was awake and knew that he was going to die. Every time I think of him, I think of the crushing fear he must have felt as the flames tore down the building around him and the smoke suffocated him.

When I first met Evan, I knew he needed a reason to live. He needed something to hold his frayed sanity together after everything he knew was torn away from him. Mrs. Alavaster introduced herself to me gently. She whispered to me that her own unbalance would help to right Evan's. Her vulnerability would help him defeat his own. The rest of the story unfolded to me like a dark room under the circle of a dying flashlight. *Silence & Song* is more about the boundaries of the human mind than it is about the crumbling boundaries of civilization.

Evan's death is both an echo and an inverse of my uncle's death. Did Evan know he was going to die? I'd like to think he didn't. And if he did, I hope that it was relief he felt and not his fear of the dark.

23
AFTERWORD

by
Robert Tozer

author of

THE ADVENTURES OF
SAWYER THOMAS

What better time to go on an epic adventure than during an apocalypse—especially if you're around twelve years old. You'd face untold perilous dangers, yet life would still continue to hold that new *start* smell to it. With Sawyer, I tried to remember and then recapture that magical time of youth - that thirst for adventure we all once had. The friends you meet, the obstacles you face, and the wonder of excitement and exploration that's as simple as riding your bike across town simply to see what's over there. I hope I succeeded in my endeavor.

THE FIRST TRUMPET

The first angel sounded his trumpet,
and there came hail and fire
mixed with blood,
and it was hurled down upon Earth.
A third of Earth was burned up,
a third of the trees were burned up,
and all the green grass was burned up.

Revelation 8:7

www.ingramcontent.com/pod-product-compliance
Lightning Source LLC
Chambersburg PA
CBHW050018180626
46810CB00002B/480